Accounting Can Be Murder

Accounting Can Be Murder

A Whodunit Award Winner

Steve McMillan

ABSOLUTELY AMAZING eBOOKS

Published by Whiz Bang LLC, 926 Truman Avenue, Key West, Florida 33040, USA.

ISBN 978-1-951150-61-7

For information contact:
Publisher@AbsolutelyAmazingEbooks.com

For Debra L
Always

Accounting
Can Be
Murder

This book was a third-place tie in the
2020 Whodunit Mystery Writing Competition

Acknowledgments

On December 23, 2019, I suffered a seizure outside of my home. After a number of tests, it was determined that I had a brain tumor that needed to be removed. While recuperating from surgery, radiation, and chemo treatments, I took the opportunity to write this novella. I would like to dedicate it to all the people who have supported me during this medical endeavor.

First, I would like to thank my many doctors. Dr. Douglas Laske, my neurosurgeon, and his staff were amazing during my surgery. Dr. Robert Lustig, my radiation oncologist, and his staff were very supportive during my radiation treatments. The coronavirus pandemic further complicated a very difficult situation, yet Dr. Lustig and his team got me through the radiation portion of my treatment. Dr. Steven Bagley, my oncologist, and his team helped me greatly in getting through the chemo portion of my treatment with minimal side effects. All of the medical staff at both Abington-Jefferson and Penn Medicine were very professional, while simultaneously being compassionate.

Second, I would like to thank a number of friends who have been there for me. Ted Kurlowicz and Roger King were instrumental in my moving quickly to take action. If not for them, I might still be getting opinions, but I wouldn't be getting better. Other supportive friends included: Rob Hamilton, Tom Stone, Deb Solfaro, Gina Kaufman, Lisa

Morris, and Gina Bachman. My ex-wife, Sue McMillan, was also very kind even as she was struggling with her own medical issue.

Next, Penn State Abington was extremely generous and considerate over these months of treatment. In particular, Dr. Damian Fernandez and Dr. Fran Sessa were very helpful and understanding.

Finally, of course, there is family. All of my kids, Emily, Mikayla, Mike, Matt, and Liam were always there for me. I knew I could count on them if I needed anything at all. Kathy Rauanheimo acted as my caregiver if at any time I was alone or needed transportation.

And naturally, there is Debbi. She schlepped me down to Penn for six weeks. She made sure I took all my medications on time. She made me special meals if my stomach was queasy. But most of all, she gave me confidence that we'll get through this. And she said we can go to both Key West and Malta when the coronavirus is over. Count on it, Honey!!

Chapter One

I really hate teaching 8 a.m. classes. The problem isn't that I'm not a morning person but more that I prefer my mornings quiet and sedate. I like to ease into the day. You might think that an eight o'clock intermediate accounting class would be very sedate, even comatose, but not the one that I have now.

I think the reason students are more involved, motivated, and enthusiastic is the current job market. They all know if they don't have the grades, they are not going to get jobs at the Big Four accounting firms. And they know that having "Big Four" on your resume opens many, many doors. So, some of them work hard and demand a lot of themselves and, sometimes, unfortunately, their professors.

Today is a particularly bad day. Yesterday was my girlfriend's birthday, and last night we went to dinner. We were supposed to go to a very intimate, exclusive, and expensive restaurant in Center City. Sharon had been pestering me to go there for months. Unfortunately, when we got there, they had lost our reservation and had no tables available for two hours. Of course, I raised hell and made a general ass of myself. In fact, the maître d' had been quite embarrassed. But that didn't get us a table. So we left, now irritable with each other since there was no one else to blame and went to a lesser restaurant that did have tables available.

Since we were ticked off in general, the meal was hardly pleasant. So we both drank too much. In fact, we drank much too much. At first, this only added to our aggravation with each other.

Sharon was angry, beyond the restaurant incident, because another birthday had come and gone, and I had not proposed. I was angry because I wanted to propose but had been so badly burned, at least in my view, in my first marriage that I could not get up the nerve. Yet I knew I was shortchanging both of us. So, two angry people sat there and drank and drank.

However, by the second bottle of wine, we had mellowed out a lot. We were so mellow that we were both slurring our words occasionally. Our anger with each other was replaced by lust. Wine tended to do that to us. So by the time we left the restaurant, we were all over each other. When we got to Sharon's, we made love until 3 o'clock in the morning. As we said goodnight, she said it was one of her best birthdays ever.

Of course, that was last night when we were both tipsy and horny and not this morning when we were both hung over and tired. Sharon is a detective with the Philadelphia Police Homicide Division. She is the only woman in the division. She is the only Jew. Thus, surprise, surprise, she is the only Jewish woman. This puts her under enormous pressure, and she drives herself very hard every single day. She hates to be in any way impaired at work. So, when she woke up with a monster headache and only three hours of sleep, someone had to be blamed. Guess who that was? So, it went from being the best birthday ever to why did I do that to her? It was a good thing that we did not spend much time together this morning.

Granted my job as an accounting professor at Temple University is not nearly as demanding as Sharon's. But I do have this aggressive, motivated 8:00 class. And today I was just not in the mood.

"Dr. Stone, I don't understand why you included Treasury stock in the earnings per share calculation. The company has held that stock for years, and it should have no bearing on their EPS," Frank Rutledge, one of my more inquisitive and abrasive students, was being particularly bothersome today.

"The reason is because the Financial Accounting Standards Board says that we must. It is a rule and rules must be adhered to in accounting. We are a profession of rules and regulations," I said.

"But this rule makes no sense. Shouldn't rules that make no sense be changed or abolished? Why do something wrong or idiotic just because that's the way we have always done it?"

Frank was not going to be easily dissuaded. My head was really starting to ache. I had had four cups of coffee but that only made me feel raw and testy. I needed to finish up class before I said something that I shouldn't. But Frank was really pressing.

"Frank, you are asking questions that I can't answer. In some of the world, they drive on the left side of the road. In the United States, we drive on the right. Maybe it doesn't make any sense to do so, but it's the way we have always done it, and it is likely that we will continue to do so," I said.

"That may be true, Professor Stone, but if we found out that the number of traffic fatalities was significantly less in countries where they drive on the left side, we would probably change to the left. This issue with Treasury stock is similar. To not include it in the calculation of EPS is clearly the more accurate method. Why doesn't the FASB just change it?"

"Tell you what, Frank; I have the FASB's address. Why don't you write a letter to them and suggest your change? Who knows, maybe no one has ever brought the discrepancy to their attention. It's called regulatory inertia. Once a rule is enacted, it's hell to change," I said.

Right then I knew I was sinking fast. Though I have been accused of occasionally having a sailor's mouth, I try diligently not to curse in class. It really is very unprofessional, even though the students usually laugh and snicker. But Frank was wearing me down. I had to get finished with class. I had to get some aspirin.

"If fact, I'll give you extra credit if the FASB changes the rule by the end of the semester," I said. Most of the class laughed out loud.

Frank doesn't have much of a sense of humor. In fact, I think comedy and laughter make him very uncomfortable. So, my little joke was the perfect ploy to shut him up. He nodded his head in resignation rather than acknowledgment and looked down at his desk.

"So, are there any other questions?" Pause for effect because I knew there would not be any. "O.K., continue in Chapter 6 for next time. I'll be working on your exams over the next few days."

As I picked up my notes, I watched the students file past. It was clear that they felt sorry for me and my obvious hangover. One student who never said anything in class smiled broadly and said, "I hope your head feels better by next class. It really looks painful."

I was beginning to understand why Sharon hated to go to work with a hangover. Not only is it painful, but it's also downright embarrassing.

Chapter Two

I was supposed to have office hours after class, but I went back to my office, waited five minutes to see if anyone would come by and left. I wasn't going to be much good to them anyway. Probably just show them the answer in the solutions manual.

Since I live in Center City, Philadelphia, I take the subway up to school and back. This is fine if I don't have a class late at night. Temple is not in the best neighborhood, and the subway gets some pretty interesting people at night. Even during the day, you never know who you might meet on the train. And, of course, these little meetings usually happen on days that you really don't want them to. Like today, for instance.

As I sat down to contemplate which of my many hangover cures I was going to use, Phil Jones bolted onto the train and plopped down beside me. Phil is an adjunct professor in accounting who has his own private tax practice. Phil is very high energy and very high volume. His classroom style is extremely animated, and students find him most entertaining. I, however, was not in the mood to be entertained, but it seemed I had little choice.

"Ben, how you doing? You look like shit. You should take better care of yourself."

"Thanks, Phil. I appreciate the commentary on my appearance and lifestyle. You have always been my icon of clean, wholesome, healthy living. What's your secret?"

Phil snickered and rolled his eyes slightly. "My secret is I don't date members of Philly's finest. You and Sharon still together?"

"Yes, we are and you're right, she is the reason I look like hell this morning. But, at my age, four hours of doing the wild thing does take a toll." I figured Phil, who is single and constantly looking for companionship, deserved some sexual ribbing.

Phil's chin dropped a bit, and he looked at me slightly askew. It was clear he momentarily believed me and was quite jealous. Then his eyes narrowed, and he smiled. "Only four? Boy, you are getting up there in years. Maybe you should eat more seafood."

We both smiled and knew we had quickly degenerated into a locker room conversation. Phil and I tend to often do this because there are is a subtle, and sometimes not so subtle, air of competition between us. An implied spirit of rivalry. Basically, this means we tell lies about our sexual prowess. And, of course, we both know they are lies.

"So, Ben, enough about your erotic escapades. How's your research on the stock market reaction to adverse auditor opinions going? Have you gotten a big enough sample yet?"

"Actually, no I haven't. It seems the market, as the popular theory goes, anticipates the adverse opinions prior to the actual announcement, and the stock prices have already adjusted. It looks like the only way I can conduct the research is to use small companies the market analysts may not follow as closely on a day-to-day basis. Of course, the journal reviewers will bitch about that. They only want to see Fortune 500 companies analyzed. But I don't know what else to do," I said.

"I wish I could help you, but you know I know very little about academic research. I get paid to teach. Of course, Temple pays me so little to do that it's a good thing I have a practice on the side," Phil said.

"Speaking of your practice, how's it going?"

"Well, you know the recession has been hard on small businesses. I've had some clients go out of business, and everyone is slow in paying. My three biggest clients have all beaten me down on my fees this year. I was at one client's office the other day and he had left a brochure from Bingham, Shore, and Co. sitting where I could see it. Just wanted me to know that if I didn't want to play ball there were others who would. You know, this accounting business used to be a profession, but now we're just sleazy bean counters," Phil said.

I laughed, but Phil was right. Accountants have always tried to take each other's clients. Anytime a partner leaves a firm he or she tries to take as many clients as possible. And a significant portion of any partner's time is spent in "practice development"; which translates as lunch, golf, and glad-handing, usually with other people's clients. But lately, accountants have really begun really snaking each other. Since few new businesses are starting, the only way to expand your practice is to take someone else's client. So, you cut your fees to new clients. Or you tell potential clients that they paid too much in tax last year (everyone thinks they did no matter how much they paid) and that you can reduce their liability this year. Or you imply their current accountants erred in some way in how they handled something. Whatever, these days it seems getting a new client justifies any means.

"Well, Phil I hope you can rebuild your practice. If I hear of anyone looking for services, I'll give them your name," I said.

"Thanks, Ben. I appreciate that, but I've always wondered why you never have started a practice on the side. You're a natural," Phil said.

"As you know I used to work in public accounting and hated it. I got out of public accounting for a reason and I have always felt that I should not even dabble in it. Plus, with the teaching, research, and service requirements for tenure, I really never had the time," I said.

"Well, I guess that's good for me; less competition. Seems everyone and their mother is hanging out a shingle as an accountant these days. Anyway, this is my stop. Nice chatting with you, Ben. See you soon," Phil said.

"Take care, Phil."

As Phil left the train, I momentarily reminisced about my public accounting days. Boy, I hated those days. And as much hell as the doctoral program at North Carolina was, it was worth it. I was finally doing something that I enjoyed. And I am good at it. I guess there is not much more you can ask of a job. Well, maybe a little more money. And no eight a.m. classes.

Chapter Three

I live in a three-story brownstone apartment not far from Rittenhouse Square. It's a great house on a great block. I have original floors and moldings, high ceilings, a deck that overlooks the city, and even a small garden. Other faculty wonder how I afford my place on a professor's salary. In fact, it's a good question. One answer is that I inherited a little money from my parents. The other answer is that I have a little money coming in on the side. But not, as most people assume, from accounting consulting. In fact, I help the Philly cops.

I assist the Philadelphia Police Department with some of their white-collar crime investigations from time to time. I realize this sounds unusual. One might ask why a 5,000-person police department would need the services of a college accounting professor. The reason is that I tend to be very lucky in criminal investigations. I always have had a great deal of success in these little escapades, starting with the very first one.

I had been dating Sharon for about three months when she asked me to look at a prospectus that she had found at a crime scene. The prospectus looked like your somewhat standard investment offering. Complex pro-formas, obtuse legalese, and a plethora of disclaimers made up the bulk of the document. However, once I went home and examined it closely, I found numerous loopholes and possible securities violations. This is not to say that any competent tax lawyer or accountant couldn't have seen the same things. But the thing I found that they might not have was a link to another murder in Seattle. And the way I made this link was purely luck.

As I was reading the prospectus, I noticed the emblem on it for recycled paper. It is quite unusual for a marketing document to be printed on recycled paper because it is usually not as glossy and much less impressive than what you get with new paper. Yet, I remembered reading something in The Wall Street Journal about a firm on the West Coast that had used recycled paper for its prospectus and received a lot of positive press for it. I tracked down the article and found it was a Seattle firm. I gave this information to Sharon who later discovered that there had also been a murder associated with this firm. With more and more sleuthing on both coasts, a link was eventually unearthed that led to uncovering a conspiracy. Both murder cases were eventually solved thanks to my recycled paper observation. This was not detective work that would impress either Sherlock Holmes or Hercule Peroit, but as the cliché goes: Sometimes it is better to be lucky than good. I tend to be very lucky, at least in this crime work.

I had hoped to go home and get a nap in so maybe I could do some work in the afternoon. But, of course, that was too much to ask for. As I was walking in the door, the phone rang.

"Hello."

"Hi, it's me. Does your head hurt as much as mine does?", said Sharon.

"Probably more, but I doubt you will believe me. In fact, I was just getting ready to take a short nap," I said.

"At 11 o'clock in the morning! Oh, to be an academic. Well, I've got something I want you to look at so you're going to have to stay up," Sharon said.

"I wonder if this is an incredible emergency or if you're just jealous that I was going to lie down," I said.

"Probably a little of both. Anyway, there was a homicide last night at a big-time Center City law firm, Dreyfuss and White. An attorney named Jon Sizemore was shot at point blank range. Cleaning crew saw him working late last night. His wife got worried when he didn't come home, and she couldn't reach him. She called the cops who got security to let them in. Of course, security didn't see anything. Found him about 2:00 a.m. Time of death was put at between 11:00 p.m. and 1:00 a.m.," Sharon said.

"That's too bad, but what am I supposed to do about it?"

"Well my, aren't we in a testy mood today. Does our widdle head hurt too much? Can we not hold our liquor? Or is it I required too much of your manly services last night?"

"Very funny. I believe my manly services made you purr last night. I've never made a woman purr before," I said.

"Shut up. I did not purr. I may have whimpered a bit, but I did not purr," Sharon said.

"Whatever you say, my precious," I said.

"God, you can be such a jerk sometimes. I really don't understand why I'm still with you," Sharon said.

"Maybe you like to purr. Excuse me, whimper," I said.

"Clown!! Anyway, why I need your help is that while we were searching the deceased's office, we found some real estate documents tucked under a drawer. We really can't understand them, and we needed an expert's opinion. And since all the experts were busy, we figured we would find out what you thought," Sharon said.

"Boy, you sure know how to sweet talk a guy. And this must be done now? It can't wait until later this afternoon?"

"Well, I suppose it could wait, but the trail gets cold very fast in murders, as you know. Hours can make a difference. Plus, if you let me come over now maybe I'll do my feline imitation for you," Sharon said.

"Well, you know they say if you take a nap during the day, you won't sleep that night. So, I guess I better go ahead and stay up. Come on by now," I said.

As I hung up, I wondered how clean the sheets were on my bed.

Chapter Four

I made a pot of coffee and waited for Sharon to come by. As many people know, the combination of coffee and hangover borders on immoral. Your hangover wants you to lie down and sleep for hours while the coffee says stay up and don't rest. It is like a war in your body. In my case, it was beginning to feel like my hangover was winning, and I didn't know if I could stay awake until Sharon got there. If I slept and she woke me up, the odds are good that I would get up grumpy. Since our last phone call seemed to have smoothed over our rough morning, I did not want to lose the momentum. Hell, maybe I even wanted to get laid again though I really couldn't understand where my desire and stamina were going to come from. So I sat down with a cup of coffee and turned on the TV.

I have only recently gotten cable. I always thought it was a waste of money since I do not watch a lot of TV. But once I went to a faculty party where the major topic of conversation was a CNN broadcast, I realized I needed to move into this century. So I ordered the basic cable.

Since I now have cable what I find amazing is how many interesting shows TV has to offer. CNN, The Financial News Network, and the Discovery Channel all offer insightful, interesting, and sometimes even challenging topics. However, my hangover was challenging me enough that day so instead I cut on MTV.

MTV is a concept that is truly amazing to me. Outside of the brief interludes with the VJ's, the entire programming is one big commercial. The videos are little more than an advertisement for the group or album involved while the standard commercials are dispersed between the videos. Almost every minute of airtime is generating income for MTV and the stations. And young kids watch this stuff for hours. As the comic Yakoff Smirnoff says, Is this a great country? My response after five minutes of MTV is: Probably not for long.

Just as I started to doze off, the buzzer rang in my apartment. I knew Sharon had her own keys and figured she was ringing the buzzer just to torture my splitting head. As I started to move toward the door, it opened, and Sharon walked in smiling.

"I hope the buzzer didn't bother you, Ben" said Sharon. "I couldn't seem to find my keys at first."

"But you seem to have found them now, you bitch," I said.

Sharon laughed loudly. She has a wonderful laugh that sounds more like a man's than a woman. It comes from her belly, and she really let it go. She told me once that her mother tried to get her to tone it down when she was a kid. It's not ladylike. But once Sharon left home, she decided she had to laugh naturally whether it was ladylike or not. Besides, as a female Jewish cop in Philadelphia, it is unlikely Sharon will be joining too many country clubs and attending many cotillions.

"So, did you bring these documents that are such an emergency with you?"

"Yes, I did," said Sharon. "And since a man was killed and these documents could be an integral part of the investigation, you could act a little less put out by my request for you to examine them."

"Sorry. You're right. Do you want some coffee while I look them over?"

"Sure, I'll get some and read the newspaper in the kitchen," she said. "I just couldn't seem to focus well enough this morning to even read the headlines."

As Sharon walked into the kitchen, I sat down and started thumbing through the accordion file she had brought. It did not take me long to figure out that most of the documents were agreements of sale for various real estate parcels in Philadelphia. The agreements were between DiAngelo Construction Company as the seller and FCL, Inc. as the buyer with Jon Sizemore signing on FCL's behalf. Most of the addresses seemed to be in the Fairmount section of Philadelphia. Real estate brokers prefer to call this the "Art Museum" area since the Philadelphia Museum of Art is not too far away. Of course, over the years what the brokers call the "Art Museum" area is no longer walking distance from the museum itself.

The Art Museum area was to have been one of the next great gentrification areas in Philadelphia. In the late '80s, the prices started to soar. Of course, compared with Center City prices, they were still affordable. But the real estate bust hit in 1990, and the market all over Philadelphia went down. The Art Museum area, which was in a state of transition, was especially hard hit. However, thumbing through the agreements of sale, it did not appear that FLC, Inc. had gotten that news.

I am not a real estate broker and do not follow the market that closely except in my immediate area. But even I knew the prices I saw were way out of line. One house had two stories with 1,500 square feet of living area that FCL, Inc. had bought for $250,000. This must be at least twice its real value. Another building, these one three stories with 2,000 square feet, was to be sold for $400,000. Again, this is at least twice the value. I was really perplexed about these mysterious transactions.

I continued to look through the documents and only found more agreements of sale. All the prices looked too high. And none of the properties were contiguous so that ruled out a company was acquiring parcels for some sort of development. As best as I could tell, FCL, Inc. was not a particularly astute real estate speculator. But then I found an even more interesting document that only added to the puzzle.

The very last document in the file was a one-page power of attorney for Jon Sizemore on behalf of FCL, Inc. As I looked to see who had endorsed the document for FCL, I almost dropped the file. Frederick C. Langritz had signed as a shareholder of FCL, Inc.

For some reason, I am seldom jealous of other people's accomplishments. Sure, I have dreamed of making the winning shot in the NBA finals or striking out Reggie Jackson with the bases loaded. But I don't envy other people and what they have done. This is not because my own ego is so large but more that I am comfortable with the choices I have made in life and feel no real competition or threat from people who have made other decisions that have led them to different, sometimes more profitable, ends. Frederick Langritz is, however, an exception to this rule.

Frederick Langritz is one of the wealthiest persons in the Delaware Valley. Of course, the Dorrance Family of Campbell Soup fame has a few bucks. And the area still has a duPont or two running around. But Langritz is up there. And what makes it even more of a Horatio Alger story is Langritz started from nothing; perhaps even less than nothing. And everyone knows the story because it has been written up so extensively in area magazines.

Langritz's father was a German Jew who came to Philadelphia in the 1930s. He started a kosher butcher shop in the Bustleton area of Northeast Philadelphia and for a period was very successful. But then Langritz's dad had a serious dispute with the chief Orthodox rabbi of Philadelphia. The rumor was that the rabbi felt Langritz was not philanthropic enough with either his time or his money in the Jewish community. Langritz allegedly told the rabbi that how he spent his personal time and money was his private business and none of the rabbi's. This proved not to be a particularly smart move since Langritz depended on the chief rabbi's kosher approval. The rabbi revoked his kosher approval, and Langritz was bankrupt in months. Langritz was in high school at this time, he thought preparing for college. But the chief rabbi short-circuited those plans.

When Langritz's dad told him that his college fund had been wiped out, he was at first upset but later relieved. Langritz has always been a lazy underachiever in school and was at best ambivalent about more schooling. Once he finished high school, he went to work for a real estate company doing odd jobs, running errands, and helping with the phone.

Langritz proved to be a quick study in real estate and soon had his broker's license. He quickly became the office's most successful agent. Then at the age of 23, he opened his own office. At 25, he opened a second office. At 27, a third and fourth. But Langritz knew that the real money is not in brokering, it is in developing. And that is what he turned to next.

Langritz developed a small strip shopping center in Northeast Philadelphia and sold it for twice its cost. He developed a 30-unit apartment complex in Queens Village and made a mint. He rehabbed an office building on Chestnut Street that sold for a small fortune. It seemed each project he was involved with was successful. But Langritz's real success proved to be in deciding that developing was not the safest way to make a lot of money in real estate. He projected the 1980s real estate boom was coming to the Philadelphia market, and he switched to land speculation. Langritz bought land all over Philadelphia. Brownstones, lots, buildings, houses, it didn't matter. He had parcels everywhere. And then he waited for the 80s.

The 80s saw real estate skyrocket in Philadelphia. The height barrier over City Hall was broken. Skyscrapers rose from the ground. Development on the Pennsylvania Convention Center began. Condo and apartment developments were everywhere. And everyone had to talk to Frederick Langritz. His name was everywhere. It seemed each time a developer was collecting parcels for a large development, Langritz had the last piece. And got the highest price. It was rumored Langritz made over $30 million on the convention center deals alone. Estimates were that Langritz's net worth moved well beyond $100 million in the 80s. But then he just stopped.

After having cashed out most of his holdings and selling his real estate offices, Langritz basically went into hiding. He has a huge estate in Gladwyne that he rarely leaves. From the rumor mill once again, he is supposedly busy writing a book, but he has not been seen in public in months. The reason I know this is that anytime he is seen, the Philadelphia Inquirer reports it as a major news item.

I guess the reason I envy Langritz a little is that he made his fortune, knew he was tired of working, quit, and now can do whatever he wants. Read, ski, sleep in (which I would have liked to have done today), or whatever. I suppose I admire the man for his willingness to check in and then out of the rat race.

"So, did you find anything interesting?" asked Sharon as she brought me a cup of coffee.

"Well, I found some real estate agreements that showed a company was paying too much for properties in the Fairmount area. And a shareholder of that company is Frederick Langritz," I said.

"The millionaire land speculator? Paying too much?"

"That's what it looks like to me," I said.

"Maybe there's a big development going up in the area," Sharon said.

"In Fairmount?" I said.

"True, it does seem unlikely. But what could that have to do with a murder?"

"I have no idea, but it's the only clue in these files."

"Well, maybe we should go talk to Langritz," said Sharon.

"I hear it's not that easy to see him. He's not exactly Howard Hughes, but he is reclusive. I'm sure we would need an appointment. I doubt we can just show up," I said.

"Oh, I don't know. My badge usually helps in these circumstances. Besides, if you call, you give them a chance to get attorneys, accountants, and who knows who else to be there to run interference. Better to just surprise them. Get those candid, unrehearsed statements. Can you come along to talk specifics once we get in?"

"O.K., but do you want to go now? I thought you had this feline thing we needed to take care of," I said.

"Ben, we are talking about a murder case. I'm on duty right now. I can't take time off for sex," Sharon said.

As I ran my hand up her thigh, I could tell she was wavering. When I reached up to massage her breast, she tried to push my hand away but not with much enthusiasm. As I reached inside her blouse, she closed her eyes and smiled.

"Well hell, here or would you like to move to the bed?" she said.

Since I knew the sheets were clean, I opted for more room to maneuver.

Chapter Five

We took the Schuylkill Expressway out to Langritz's home. Fortunately, we were traveling during the late afternoon because the Schuylkill becomes a parking lot around 4:00 p.m. I abhor commuting, which is one of the reasons I have always lived downtown. Even though my hours are somewhat flexible, there are times I would have to travel during rush hour and the idea of sitting in traffic is nauseating. It has always amazed me how far people will commute on a regular basis. I read someplace that there are colleges in the New York area that offer classes on the commuter trains.

There is a group of about 75 people who take Amtrak from 30th Street Station every morning up to Manhattan. They have turned it into a sort of club and even socialize with each other on weekends. But, as much as I'm sure these are very nice people, this is not a club to which I aspire to join.

We turned off on the Gladwyne exit. As we were winding our way through all the multimillion-dollar houses, we both looked at each other and smiled.

"Neat thing. Give your house a name," I said.

"Maybe you should try it?"

"Chateau de Stone? Ben Villa?"

"How about just the Love Shack," said Sharon.

"Probably have to clear it with the B-52s," I said. "But am I to take it from that comment that we have completely reconciled from this morning?"

"Maybe, depends on where you take me for dinner tonight."

"I have to buy your affection!"

"Actually, you can only rent it for a while and it's very expensive. Pizzeria Uno takeout," Sharon said.

"That I can probably handle."

As we turned onto Langritz's street the houses got even larger, and they were pretty big already. They were now all set back from the street hidden from the road by bushes, trees, and exotic flowers. We tried to look for house numbers but couldn't find any. I guess if you have to ask you don't belong there.

We turned up one driveway and drove the two city blocks until we got to the house. There was a gardener in the front yard mowing the grass. Sharon leaned out her window and called to him.

"Hi! I'm a cop, and I need directions to a house on this street?"

The man stared at her. "No hablo Ingleis, senorita."

Sharon looked at me and smiled. I have a little Spanish, which was much more than she has. I got out of the car and went around to the front of the car. I tried to look friendly so the gardener would be less nervous.

I said, "Por favor, donde esta la casa de Langritz?"

The gardener began speaking very quickly and gesturing with his hands. I couldn't follow anything he said so I told him to stop. I couldn't remember the word for driveway, so I pointed to it. The gardener nodded that he understood.

I walked to the edge of the driveway and pointed to the right and said, "Si?"

The gardener smiled that he understood and said, "Si."

I turned to the right and pointed out to my side with my left arm. "Si."

"No, dereche."

"Cuantos?" and I pointed to the driveway.

The gardener thought for a moment and said, "Cinco."

"Muchas gracias."

I got back into the car. "We go right out of the driveway and it's the fifth driveway on the right. By the way, good thing you didn't show him your badge. He probably would have thought you were ICE and run."

"True. Think his employer pays the appropriate payroll taxes?" Sharon said.

"Probably not. But then again maybe he doesn't want to be attorney general someday."

We then drove down to the fifth driveway on the right. As we turned in, there is a locked iron gate with an intercom on the left. We pulled up to the gate, and Sharon leaned out the window and pressed the intercom button.

In about 10 seconds, a voice with a heavy British accent says, "May I help you?"

"This is Detective Levin of the Philadelphia Police Homicide Division. I would like to speak to Mr. Langritz for a few minutes if possible."

"What may I say is the issue?"

"Tell Mr. Langritz that this is just a routine investigation, but that it is important that I speak to him."

"One moment, please."

It took longer than a moment. In fact, it took almost 15 minutes before the voice came back on the intercom.

"Mr. Langritz informs me that he would prefer not to speak to you since you have no jurisdiction in this area, and he does not have an attorney present."

Sharon peeved from the 15-minute wait and having to think fast said, "Fine. I'll get a warrant, send it to the Lower Merion police, and we'll see Mr. Langritz downtown. I'm sure he'll enjoy the experience. You meet such a wonderful class of people at downtown police headquarters."

Sharon was bluffing. There was almost no way, based on what we currently had for evidence, to get a warrant. And whether the Lower Merion police would cooperate was far from a sure thing. But she sounded very sincere. And sincerity is key to carrying out a bluff.

We could hear voices in the background. One voice sounded very angry. The British voice seemed to be trying to calm the other down with little success. But Sharon's bluff had the desired effect.

"Mr. Langritz can see you for only ten minutes."

"Fine," said Sharon. "I'm sure it will not take any longer than that. Please open the gate."

A loud buzzer sounded, and the gate began opening. When it was completely open, we drove through.

I said, "You would think a big deal real estate developer like Langritz would see through a bush league ruse like that warrant thing."

"Bush league? I thought it sounded very genuine," said Sharon, "But you're right. Why would he fall for something so obvious?"

"The answer is that he didn't. Maybe he just wants to talk. Papers say he doesn't get out much. Maybe he has something to hide and wants to see what we know," I said. "Or maybe he has high-powered binoculars and could see how that blouse strains across your chest."

Sharon giggled. "You're right. I shrank this one in the dryer. I thought no one would notice. Why did you let me wear it out this morning?"

"This morning I could hardly see to the end of my nose. To be honest, I just noticed it. But now that I do, I sort of like it. I bet the guys at work do, too."

"Thanks, just what I do not need down at headquarters is all the guys leering at my tight blouse. It's hard enough to be taken seriously without something like that. I'll have to stop at home on my way back to the office."

We drove for what seemed to be 15 minutes up to the house. As we came over the top of a small hill, we got our first look at Langritz's home. It was truly fabulous. A French chateau with three stories and at least 30 rooms. Ivy covered over half the front. A small detached house sat about 30 yards from the main one. The circular driveway enclosed a lily pad garden that appeared to be stocked with luminescent fish.

Sharon said, "Nice digs. Think you could ever set us up in something like this?"

"If you mean the servant's quarters over there, maybe. That is, if you would be willing to homestead in the Parkside area of Philly. There is some amazing architecture very similar to this over there."

"There are also some amazing drug addicts, muggers, and other assorted criminals. If that's the best you can do, I'll think I'll pass," said Sharon.

"No sense of adventure."

"More like not enough life insurance." After parking the car, we walked up to the somewhat massive door and rang the bell. The door was so thick that we couldn't hear a thing. But apparently someone inside could because in a moment the door opened and a very properly dressed man appeared.

"Lt. Levin, I assume," he said in that very British accent we had heard over the intercom. "You did not mention that you were not alone."

"This is my associate, Dr. Stone. He is involved in this investigation at the request of the Philadelphia police and is acting in a very official capacity. It is critical that he be present when I speak to Mr. Langritz."

"Very well, please come in."

The room that we entered was truly breathtaking. The ceiling was at least 20 feet high. The walls appeared to be mahogany. The carpet we stood on was at least 50 by 50 feet. A huge staircase was directly in front of us that had a three-inch-thick Oriental carpet all the way up. Sculpture, original paintings, and tapestries lined the walls. I thought I recognized a Matisse. Very, very impressive.

"Please wait here. I must inform Mr. Langritz of Mr. Stone's presence since Mr. Langritz agreed only to see Lt. Levin."

"That's Dr. Stone," I said.

"Yes, of course. Dr. Stone. Please wait here." He disappeared through a heavy, thick door.

While we waited, Sharon and I walked around the room. The walls had hand-carved etchings all over them. The tables were mostly marble topped. A close-up view of the artwork confirmed how impressive it really was. The suspected Matisse was one. The question of whether it was an original did not even cross my mind. Sharon bent and touched the rug. She whistled. The cost of the chandelier that hung from the ceiling might have fed a small country for a few days. Langritz certainly knew how to live.

"Sure, you can't afford something like this?" Sharon said.

"If I could afford something like this, my fantasy night with Cindy Crawford would probably come true."

"Yeah, well, I'll keep her ex Richard Gere busy while you entertain Cindy."

We both were smiling at each other when the butler returned. He did not seem in a particularly festive mood.

"Mr. Langritz has agreed to see you, but I must say he is most unhappy about the addition of Mr., uh, Dr. Stone. Mr. Langritz finds this whole situation most distressing and does not like surprises."

Sharon spoke up. "Yes, well, we will try to be brief. As I said, it is only routine."

"Very well, come this way."

We walked through the heavy door and down a hall. We entered what appeared to be the library. The walls being lined with leather-covered books from top to bottom sort of gave it away. Large deep chairs were spread throughout the room. A fireplace burned in the corner. I looked down at some of the most beautiful Oriental rugs I had ever seen.

As we made our way across the vast expanse of the room, Sharon leaned over and whispered, "Something like this would be nice, Stone. I think you should ask for a raise."

"Double my salary, and we might be able to buy half of this rug we're walking across."

Frederick Langritz had his back to us as we approached. As he turned, I could see why he had a reputation as a fierce negotiator. He stood at least six feet four and weighed about 225. His hair was a thick salt and pepper, and his face was barely wrinkled with a strong Roman chin. He looked like a very worthy opponent in any endeavor, and he did not look pleased to see us.

"Dr. Stone. Lt. Levin." He did not extend his hand.

Sharon decided to open the conversation. "Mr. Langritz, I am sorry to disturb you like this, but it will only take a few moments of your valuable time," she said.

"No, Lt. Levin. You are not sorry to disturb me. You wanted to catch me off-guard and without the benefit of counsel. So, please ask your questions so that you may leave."

It didn't seem like we were getting off to a very good start.

Chapter Six

Even though it was clear Langritz was not happy to see us and wanted us to hurry, he gestured at two chairs for us to take. He then sat in a very large one across from us. Didn't seem like he was going to offer refreshments though. Sharon decided to get things started.

"Mr. Langritz, I must assume that you have heard about the murder downtown last night in the offices of Dreyfuss and White. A Mr. Jon Sizemore was killed."

"Yes, I saw that on the news this morning. Such a tragedy for someone so young, but what does that have to do with me?" queried Langritz.

I decided I should jump in. "Well, the police found a number of legal documents in Mr. Sizemore's office, and they found one that referenced you. It was about something called FCL, Inc. We wanted to know if you could tell us anything about the company and what it did."

"Dr. Stone, as I am sure you know, I have been basically retired for a number of years now. In fact, I have spent most of my time on philanthropic activities. I'm sure there are still some entities floating around that have my name associated with them, but I really am not aware of any of their current activities."

I decided I better press a little. "Well, this particularly entity has been very active in buying houses in the Art Museum area, at what I think are vastly inflated prices. And Mr. Sizemore had a power of attorney document from you that was dated less than two years ago. Are you sure that you don't remember anything about FCL?"

"Dr. Stone, I sign a great many documents even in my retirement, and while I try to be thorough in reviewing them all, I'm sure there are some that slip through. I rely on my lawyers and accountants to make sure all my activities are legal and properly accounted for. Perhaps it would be best if you spoke to my primary attorney?"

Sharon chimed back in. "I'm sure that would be helpful, but since this is a murder investigation and right now one of the few leads we have concerns FCL, it's important that we get as much information from you as possible."

"As I told you, I have not been active in business in many years. I still have some holdings that I never liquidated, but I do not keep a close eye on any of it. As far as new developments are concerned, I occasionally see things that might interest me, but, again, I haven't been done much in years. Also, and I assume you are somewhat familiar with how I made my fortune, a group of likely modest houses in the Art Museum area would hardly be worth my time even during my heyday of development. I really don't know how much I can add to what I've said."

Sharon noted, "Well, you could perhaps authorize your accountants and lawyers to provide us with information about your FCL Holdings?"

"I'm not a lawyer, but wouldn't a warrant be necessary before I did that?"

I said, "That's quite true, but it seems that you have nothing to hide, so perhaps you could expedite the process by allowing access without a warrant. We can certainly get a warrant, but since everything is kosher in your mind, why make us do so?"

"Fine, I will have my assistant, Joan Buster, contact my counsel and accountants to gather the information you require. I don't know how long it will take, but I will courier the information to Lt. Levin's office. Will that suffice?"

Sharon said, "Sure, that would be a great start, but could you have Ms. Buster provide us with the names, addresses, etc. of your lawyers and accountants? We would like to follow up with them in a few days to see how things are going."

"Fine, I'll have her get the relevant information tomorrow and email it to you. Is there anything else that you need?"

"No, that will be sufficient right now, and we certainly appreciate your time, Mr. Langritz. It's been nice to meet you. I have been a fan for years," I said.

"Well, this encounter has not made me a fan of you, Dr. Stone, and even less of Lt. Levin, and I hope that we never meet again."

Guess we won't be getting a holiday card from him anytime soon. Oh, well, at least I got to see his house.

Chapter Seven

So, Sharon had a very early morning the next day. While I was tempted to sleep in, I figured I might as well do some grading since we were waiting to hear from Langritz's assistant about his documents concerning FCL.

While, in general, I enjoy the teaching, and even the research, aspect of my job, the grading is just really a drag. Because of the nature of my classes being accounting, it's not so easy to just do multiple-guess exams with Scantrons you run through the scanner. I suppose that I could just do problems that students work on, find the right answer, and then pick the right answer from the multiple-guess choices. However, it's easy to mess up, particularly under the pressure of an exam, on a simple math calculation while really understanding the general gist of the question. I've always thought that is a bit unfair, so I must grade each problem and give partial credit for the process even if the final answer it not absolutely correct.

Actually, I guess I don't have to do it that way, but I did my MBA in accounting at The American University in DC, and most of my profs there did problem sets and gave partial credit. I did have one who only had us fill out Scantron forms based on the questions he asked. But that worked totally in my favor.

That professor taught auditing and accounting theory. He ran his own CPA review class, and he used his materials from that for our classes at AU. What was funny was that he used a CPA review guide developed by a group named Gleim and Delaney. He told us using the review guide would assist in our preparation for his tests. Pretty much only me took him seriously.

I bought an older version of the review guide to help prepare. It had hundreds of multiple-choice exam questions. I looked at all of them figuring it would be helpful. Then, I got a shock.

When we were given the first exam for the first test I had in his class, I quickly noticed that the questions were verbatim from the review guide. Not just close, but the same. I had to pretend that I was looking at the test for at least a half-hour because I was done with the test in ten minutes.

I got a great score on that test, and on all the other ones that I had in this guy's classes. His approach never wavered no matter the course or the exam. I just kept using the review guide and kept getting high scores on all of his exams.

I'll admit that at times I felt a little guilty, not because of using the test guides as he recommended them, but because I never told any of my classmates what I had discovered. But, just like all professional degrees, MBA programs are ruthlessly competitive. I was the only MBA student in my class who graduated with a perfect 4.0 average. And while I might have done so regardless, having the inside info about my accounting classes surely helped my GPA. Yeah, I felt a little guilty, but I got over it very quickly.

So I had a very big stack of intermediate accounting exams to grade. It was their second test, so I had some idea of which students were likely to do well and which ones would not. It's sort of funny how academia has changed in the years I had been at Temple. When I first started, I usually had a normal curve type of distribution. I tended to grade a little high, but the bell curve was close. Now it seems I have a bimodal distribution. I have some very hardworking students who do great in the class, and I have several them who suck. And this seems to be consistent each year and with each class. I've tried to encourage the low performers to study harder and prepare better, but it just doesn't seem to matter to a large part of the class. I don't know if they're wealthy, slick, or just don't care, but it just doesn't seem to change.

I was just pulling up the first exam when I got a call from Sharon.

"Hi, sweetness, guess what we got delivered just a few minutes ago?"

"We got the Langritz documents already?"

"Yep, but it's just the list of his accountants and lawyers. He has just one accounting firm, Teti and Company, but he's got a boatload of lawyers, however, according to his assistant, only one law firm worked on the FCL project: Dreyfuss and White, the office where the murder took place.

Wow, Dreyfus and White is one of the premier law firms in Philadelphia. That Langritz would be using them is not surprising, but, using them for a relatively modest project like this one is unusual. Dreyfus and White bills at $750 an hour, and some overpriced homes in the Art Museum area couldn't stand too much of that billing rate. I had just figured that the files on Sizemore's desk had been sent over from a cheaper firm just to be included in Langritz's overall legal position.

The choice of Teti and Company was also a bit unusual. Teti is a solid mid-level local accounting firm, but one would think that Deloitte, KPMG or Ernst and Young would be the choice. It's a little weird with a topflight old white-shoe law firm coupled with a mid-level local accounting firm. It happens, but not very often.

I asked Sharon, "How long do we give them to send us the documents before we start bugging them?"

"I guess we could give them four or five days. I'm sure they have the files; it's just getting them scanned or copied and getting them to us."

"Then what do we do in the meantime?"

"We could start by examining the FCL documents that are on file."

"Those are really just agreements of sale for a bunch of houses in the Art Museum area. Nothing seemed that unusual except the prices of the houses and the surprising power of attorney. We really need to see the corporate and partnership documents, as well as the financial statements to make any serious headway."

"So basically, you're going to sit on your ass for a few days doing what?"

"Grading, darling, the bane of my existence."

Chapter Eight

Three days later, I got an early morning call from Sharon. "We have all the documents from both the accountants and the lawyers. Should I send them over by messenger, or should I come over myself with them?"

"Why don't you come over for lunch? You can bring the documents, and we can break bread together."

"Nooner?"

"Maybe, but we had quite the romp last night, and I'm getting a little old for such a rapid turnaround."

"That's a little sad, but I could pick up some decent deli food on my way, and we could start looking at what we have. As I'm sure you can imagine, there is a lot to go through."

"Sounds great. Get me the usual Rueben sandwich and some fries. Need some comfort food before we start this little endeavor."

"Not a problem. I'll see you between noon and 12:30."

Since I had some time to kill, I decided to look at the grades that I had done over the last few days. It takes a lot of time to grade these practice sets and problems, but it's really the right way to do it. I had finished most of the grading, but I had to figure out what types of grades, and maybe curves, I was going to use.

Between my two classes of intermediate accounting, I had 64 students. The average raw score for the 64 was a 72. In the Temple grading scale, that would be a C-, which is a little bit low. The problem was that just like has happened many times lately, I had a very bimodal distribution. I had twenty students who had a ninety or above average. Then, I had twenty-five with a sixty-five or below, which is failing in the Temple grading world. To get the low end up to at least passing as a C- or

D, the upper end would be almost entirely scaled to 100 percent. I really couldn't do that as I'm sure I would hear something from my department chair about being too easy. It's true that I'm tenured, so there is not much they can do, but I don't like having the hassle. In the end, I decided that I could curve the raw scores up seven points, which got the low end up to a C- and kept the top end from all getting perfect scores. It wasn't a perfect system, but I try to be as fair as I can, even though many students don't deserve to pass the class. But I've always felt that even if they pass my classes, either intermediate two or the CPA exam will make up for it. Yeah, I'm passing the buck off to someone else, but that's okay, I can live with it.

I was just entering my grades on my grade book at about 11:30 when I got a knock at the door. I figured it was Sharon who got there a bit early, but she has a key to my door, so why would she knock?

I opened the door, and was surprised to find a tall, rather beefy fellow standing outside. I didn't recognize him, so I just said, "Hello, how can I help you?"

"You are Dr. Ben Stone." he said with a very thick Italian accent.

"Yes, I am. What can I do for you?"

"My name is Angelo Bartonelli, and I was wondering if you have a few moments to speak with me? It's regarding FCL, Inc."

"Sure, but I have an appointment with Lt. Sharon Levin of the Philly police at any moment as she is bringing over documents about FCL."

"Then, maybe I should just speak to you right now at your door."

"Okay, but that seems a little weird."

Bartonelli leaned into a doorway and stared straight into my face. It was clear he was trying to bully me a bit, but I couldn't figure out why.

"Well, Dr. Stone, it's simple. I represent some of the FCL shareholders, and they would very much like you to limit your investigation of FCL. Toward that end, they have authorized me to give you $10,000 in cash which I have in my pocket."

I was shocked. Totally taken aback. The guy just comes right out and offers me a bribe. Even does it in broad daylight, on my front porch.

"That's a very nice offer, but I don't understand. I haven't even begun my investigation of FCL: I have no idea what is there or not there."

"I understand, but my associates would just like to make sure that there are no legal issues coming up with your investigation."

"Actually, that's a good question. How did you and your associates find out about me anyway? I haven't even been involved with the case until a few days ago."

"We have our sources, and what does it matter? I'm offering you $10,000 to just not look too deeply into FCL. It's easy money."

I paused and then said, "Actually, it's not so easy as I do a lot of work with the Philly police, and Lt. Levin is a close friend, so it's not so simple as just doing a lousy job on the investigation. There are other factors involved."

Bartonelli leaned even closer into me. I could almost smell his cigar breath.

"Okay, let me make it simple since we have little time. I would strongly encourage you to accept the 10 large. My associates and I have other means by which we might inspire more cooperation from you and even Lt. Levin. Trust me, taking the money is much better than the alternatives."

I stood there completely dumbstruck. In a matter of maybe five minutes, he had attempted to bribe and then threaten me. I'd worked with the cops for a while, and I knew a lot of stories from Sharon, but this was just nuts. I honestly could not think of anything to say. That was fine as Bartonelli was ready to go.

"How about we do it this way? I'll come back about the same time tomorrow. Give you a little time to think about it. I'll have the money in my hand, and I sincerely hope you decide to take it. If not, we will likely have a third meeting under less congenial circumstances. Give Lt. Levin my best."

He quickly turned away and headed out to the street. I've had some strange things happen both as a professor and an accountant, but this was the top of the list. I just stood there looking at him leave and wondering what the hell I was going to say to Sharon when she got there. I was especially ready for her to get there with her gun. That is certainly never an emotion I had had with her before. But, the last ten minutes were chocked full of first times.

Chapter Nine

I was just sitting on my sofa staring at the wall, when Sharon walked in. She was carrying a sack of food in one hand and a large briefcase in the other.

"So, I got your rueben and fries. I also got you a large soda to wash it all down."

I just continued to sit there staring at the wall. Sharon looked at me with a level of concern.

She said, "What's wrong? Are you sick or something? Why are you just sitting there?"

I continued to just sit, but after a moment, I was able to at least respond.

"I just got offered a bribe and a threat all within about five minutes."

"What the hell are you talking about?"

"Right before you arrived, I had a guest named Angelo Bartonelli who offered me 10 thousand dollars to tank the FCL investigation, and then suggested that if I didn't do it, the next choice to assure compliance would be much less attractive than a bunch of money."

"Have you been early morning drinking, or even still hung over from last night? You can't be serious about what you just said."

"Oh, I am very serious and very much shaken up about it. We haven't even started looking at FCL and I've already been bribed and threatened. You're going to have to give me a minute to collect myself."

Sharon sat down on the sofa next to me and put her hand on my shoulder to try to comfort me. I just sat there and tried to breath in as much air as I could. After a couple of minutes, I finally thought I could actually speak.

"So, let me run through what actually transpired. I was just sitting at the kitchen table having some coffee. About 11:30, the doorbell rang. I thought it might be you, but you have a key, although I thought you might have your hands full and used your arm to ring the bell. I went to the door, opened it, and there was this fairly good-sized guy standing in front of me. As I said, he introduced himself as Angelo Bartonelli and that he represents some of the investors in FCL. He then offered me 10K in cash, and when I hesitated, he suggested the next step might be much less attractive. I told him you were due to arrive soon, so he suggested I take a day to think about it, and that he will return about this time tomorrow. He left, and I sat down on my sofa and waited for you."

"Are you serious? What the hell is going on?"

"I wish I knew, but I'm giving you the facts, and that's about all I can do."

Sharon could tell that I was really shaken up, and rather than jumping into what the next steps might be, she leaned over and just hugged my shoulders. We just sat there for about five minutes. I didn't feel like crying, or even screaming, but I really didn't know how I was supposed to feel. Numb comes to mind, but I was far too anxious for that to be the choice.

Sharon decided to let me make the first move. "Okay, I'm somewhat together now, so you can start asking questions. I know you have a lot you want to say."

Sharon responded, "No, whatever police-like things I have can wait. I want to know if you are okay or if I need to call 911 or take you to a hospital. Even with what little you have said, this is a lot to handle, and I want to know if you're physically okay.?

"No, I'm not having a heart attack, and yes, I am a bit lightheaded, but I don't need 911 or the hospital. Maybe a glass of water would be good. I'm ramped enough that coffee would be overkill."

Sharon got up and went to the kitchen. She got a glass, put some ice in it, and then filled it with water from my refrigerator. She came back over to the sofa, handed it to me, and then sat back down on the sofa.

I sipped the water and continued to breath in deeply. I started to feel much more in control of myself but also felt like I still had a ways to go. Finally, I said to Sharon that I was able to discuss what happened.

She said, "Okay, take your time. There is no hurry. I'll call the office and tell them that I'm doing a first glance of the FCL documents with you."

"Well, as you know, the morning started out fine. You and I had a plan for lunch and the FCL documents. Then this guy Bartonelli shows up and all hell breaks loose."

"So, was he at all clear about what he wanted?"

"Pretty clear that he didn't want me looking too closely at the FCL documents. I told I hadn't even started yet, and I had no idea what I might find. Naturally, my first thought was that there must be something there or why would he be at my home. And I inquired as to how he even knew that I was even involved in this investigation. His response was that he and his associates know people involved in FCL."

Sharon responded, "Well, people at the station know about you, but it seems unlikely that's their source. The only other person who knows anything about you is Langritz and his staff."

"I figured the same thing, but I just can't see how he would care that much about this thing. As he told us, even if he were somehow intimately involved in FCL, it's just not enough money to get his attention."

"Well, if you think you're up to it, why don't we go ahead and have lunch, and then we can figure out what we are doing tomorrow when this guy returns. But, instead of the soda I brought over, might be time to break out the Chablis."

"Works for me!!"

Chapter Ten

After a little lunch and a good bit of Chablis, we finally decided to sit down and figure out what our next move was going to be.

I started, "Well, I guess the first question is what am I going to do tomorrow?"

"There are a number of options. First, you could just not be here. That's the easiest choice. Not much he can do about that, but you probably don't want to leave your house indefinitely, so it's likely just a matter of time before he makes contact."

"That's not very attractive. A lot of uncertainty and basically waiting around."

"I tend to agree, plus I would like to have more control over the situation. Second, I could just be here when he contacts you, waive my badge and gun, and he will probably leave. The problems with that approach are that we don't gather any intelligence about what this is about, and it's extremely likely that he might follow through with whatever his threat meant, plus we again are not in control."

"Same level of attraction as the first choice. I hope your third or fourth choice gets better."

"You take the money!"

"What do you mean: Take the money."

"No, you play along with this guy. You tell him that you really don't think there's much in FCL, tell him you took a quick glance, and it's doesn't look like anything big is there, but you'll still take the money."

I responded, "But am I not committing some sort of crime?"

"Nope, you are assisting the Philadelphia Homicide Division with a murder investigation. I'll draw up a short memo to that effect. You'll be in the clear legally."

"But, why would I want to play along? Why would I give this guy what he wants?"

"Because that puts us in control. He has no idea how much info you can sift out of the documents. He will have no idea how much info you are sharing with me. By the way, when he asks tomorrow, you decided quickly that you liked the money, so you didn't tell me anything about this whole deal."

"That's your master plan. I take a bribe from a thug, look the other way on the FCL documents, and hope that I live to see my next birthday."

Sharon chuckled, "Ben, I'm not throwing you to the wolves, or even the mob. I think the best thing we can do is try to keep this Bartonelli guy out of your way as much as we can, do our own due diligence in private, and then we figure out the next steps. I know it may sound nuts, but it's probably the best way to keep you safe, at least for now. If I could think of a better way, I'd do it, but I really think this is the best approach.'

Since Sharon has a lot more experience with this than I do, I really don't have much of a leg to stand on, but I was still a little nervous. Taking a bribe from a mob character is not my idea of a great plan.

"Yep, that's the plan. I'll hide in the backroom tomorrow just in case something goes wrong, but I'll try to be quiet like a mouse. In fact, I think the best thing we can do right now is take a little break, maybe watch something on TV to clear our heads, eat some more if you want, and then start sorting through these documents I have."

"Okay, that's a good idea, but we're not watching *Goodfellas* or *The Godfather*. In fact, I think a cricket match, something I don't understand at all, would a good distraction."

Chapter Eleven

We finally decided on about 30 minutes of *NCIS* as a way to clear our heads. We had seen the episode so just watching half of the show was fine. It didn't really make me feel great, but I was certainly doing better than an hour before. We sat down at my dinner table, and Sharon spread out the documents from her briefcase.

She began with saying, "The legal documents came in first. They are the pile on the left. The financial information is the stack on the right, and they go back about three years."

"Let's start with the financial info since that more my area of expertise than the legal stuff."

"Fine, I'll call the office and see if someone can run some background on Bartonelli."

Sharon handed me the stack of financial stuff, and I started to look through them. FCL was set up as a Subchapter S corporation, meaning that as long as there are fewer than 100 partners, the entity is provided with the benefits of incorporation while being taxed as a partnership. I also noticed that in addition to the tax returns, FCL had financial statements prepared probably because their banks or other financial institutions required them.

What first caught my attention was that my initial scan of the previous documents suggested that FCL had overpaid for its properties was correct. FCL had not made any money in the three years I had to examine. In fact, it looked like most of the properties were sitting empty. Between the closing costs of the properties and depreciation, on a tax basis FCL's financial position pretty much sucked.

Because of the differences between tax and financial rules, their financial statements looked a little better. Still lost money, but as much as on a tax basis. What really struck me was I still couldn't see why Langritz or anyone like him would make such stupid investments. The properties still weren't contiguous, so that ruled out a big development being considered. It was just a bunch of overpriced houses sitting in various parts of the Art Museum area.

But then I noticed something that looked a little weird. Almost all the houses on the FCL financial statements and its tax returns, were still on the books. However, there had been two parcels sold to a group called Art Museum Associates. What was really unusual was that these houses had been sold for a substantial premium over their original prices. Since I thought the original price was way too high, these numbers were completely outrageous. In fact, one house on Fairmount Avenue sold for almost three times what I would consider a reasonable price. I'm not sure what it means, but it seems to mean something.

I decided I would bring Sharon up to speed, since she had been waiting quietly for a while after she made her call to the precinct.

"So, I gave the financials a quick look. Other than confirming what I thought about the prices paid, there is one other unusual thing. There are two properties that FCL sold to another party for substantially more than the inflated prices FCL paid. But other than figuring that FCL and this other group, Art Museum Associates, are just bad business people, I don't really know what to make of it."

"Well, you're the accounting expert, not me, but I do know enough about real estate to say that people buy houses for all sorts of reasons, and sometimes they just make mistakes. Are you sure this isn't some kind of gathering of parcels to then demo and build condos or the like?"

"Maybe, but the current houses are all over the place, and a lot of houses not currently owned would need to be bought before any sort of development might occur. I mean a lot of houses. Just doesn't seem to make sense to me."

"Nothing else seemed out of place on the financials?"

"Not really. Just buying houses and leaving them vacant, no renters or the like, makes for a pretty simple tax return. Not much financial magic can be done. The only game you could play would be with depreciation and amortization, but the houses have to be occupied for that to happen. Right now, all I see is that FCL has a lot of cash, there are no mortgages on the properties, and they don't seem to be in much of a hurry to make any profit, other than the two they sold to Art Museum Associates. Oh, and since they have no mortgages, I'm not sure why they did the financial statements, but maybe the shareholders just wanted to see them. Since there's not a lot of action, the financials are pretty easy and cheap to do."

"So, in essence, you've got nothing."

"That's not quite true. I've got some overpriced houses, and two really overpriced ones. You're right, I don't know what it means, but it must be something."

"Well, do you want to try the legal documents and see if they help?"

"Sure, it can't hurt, and maybe it can shed some light."

Pulling out the legal papers, I started with the articles of incorporation. Looked like FCL had a number of different shareholders, none of whom I recognized. Most of the articles looked pretty boilerplate to me, in fact I was puzzled why a big-time law firm like Dreyfus and White would be handling something so trivial, although the "bill them till they bleed" mantra at most big firms meant that as long the client paid, they would do the work.

I thought that one place for Sharon to start would be to run a background check on the partners. She could do that from police headquarters. Give her something to do, and also maybe provide some info that would be useful.

"By the way, did the crime scene investigators find anything yet?" I asked Sharon.

"Not much. Everything had been wiped clean. Desk, chair, etc. Couldn't find any hair fibers or the like on the victim. The medical examiner ran the ballistics and we're looking at a .45 caliber hollow point. Execution-style which probably means there was a silencer. To be honest, we don't have much to go on right now. The medical examiner will do some more tests, just to be sure, but it seems to be just what it looks like: The execution of a junior associate at a big-time law firm late at night. I had no idea that the legal business was so dangerous."

"Well, given my new buddy, Mr. Bartonelli, I had no idea that academia and accounting were so dangerous. Anything on Bartonelli yet?"

"I had them run the name through the databases, and it shouldn't be a big surprise that there is more than one Angelo Bartonelli in the Philadelphia area. In fact, there are five. When I get back to the precinct, I'll pull up some pictures and send them over to you to see if your new buddy is one of them."

"So, just to refresh my recollection, the plan for tomorrow is to just take the money, and promise that I'll not look to deeply into the financials?'

"Yep, I'll be right here, with my gun, in case he decides he wants to change the deal. Hopefully, one of the pictures I send you will give us a little more info about him before he gets here."

"Then, why don't you head back to your office and get those up on a screen if you can. I'd feel a lot better if I knew a little about this guy before I commit a major felony on his behalf."

"Sure, I'll head back and try to do a little reconnaissance on Mr. Bartonelli. I'll email you over any pictures that I can find."

"Thanks. I'll just take some time and stare at these documents to see if anything catches my eye."

As she left, Sharon looked at me closely and said, "Don't worry, honey. We can work this whole thing out." Then, she gave me a quick kiss on the lips.

"I naturally trust you, but I wish I were as confident as you are. But, having a plan is better than not having one. I'll be here when you have any more intel about the Bartonelli clan."

With that, Sharon opened the door, blew me a second kiss, and was out the door. I locked my doors, checked them again to see they were locked, and pulled on the doorknob just to be sure. Best to be thorough when dealing with possible mobsters.

Chapter Twelve

While I waited to see if Sharon had anything on Bartonelli, I figured I would go through the FCL documents again. To be honest, I didn't think there was that much going on other than overpriced houses, but there had to be something for Bartonelli to offer 10 grand.

I figured I would start back with the tax returns and financial statements. The tax returns were still pretty straightforward, so I thought I might look at the shareholders. There were only four, and none of the names jumped out at me as memorable. But then I figured maybe if I Googled their names it might shed some light.

A search of the first three shareholders really didn't yield any particular insight. All three showed up on Google, but just as local real estate investors, and nothing really useful. However, number four looked a little more interesting.

John Delullo was also a real estate man, but the search also showed some articles about trouble he had had. From a Philadelphia Inquirer article from the late 1990s, there was a piece about Delullo being involved in a conspiracy to defraud a number of his real estate clients. Apparently, he had set up a number of shell corporations to try to hide the fact that some houses he had sold had been acquired under somewhat dubious circumstances. The article indicated that Delullo used money he was accused of deriving from bribes to assist with various types of political assistance in the Philadelphia area. One example was for getting the approvals from the city government for an urban development action grant. The

UDAG was to help with the financing for a large retail center in Center City. Local government needed to sign off so the grant application could go to the federal government. Delullo was accused of shaking down the developer of the property and using the money to buy a number of houses through the shell corporations. The article indicated that Delullo set up the shell corps in an attempt to launder the money he allegedly received from the developer.

The clip centered on the idea that while there was a lot of circumstantial evidence against Delullo, there wasn't a smoking gun. His explanation was that he had flipped a number of empty houses during the 1980's, and that's where the money came from. The district attorney pulled all those files, and there were many inconsistencies between what Delullo said and the actual documents. But there still wasn't enough to indict Delullo criminally, just to try to go after him for tax evasion. Even that proved hard to do because at the time tax law was written that such that the burden of proof was on the prosecution, not on the defendant. Delullo paid some pretty hefty fines, but not much else went down.

As I was reaching to put the files away, I suddenly had a light come on in my head. Well, maybe not a light, but a flicker of one. Ever since I had first met Langritz, I couldn't for the life of me figure out why he was involved with such a puny investment in the Art Museum area. But, now the Delullo slant may make the whole thing a little more understandable. Maybe Langritz had been involved with Delullo in one of his schemes. Then, I shook my head and thought, "Come on, Langritz was already a retired multimillionaire by the 90s. There is absolutely no reason that he would be involved with this type of scheme." But it was about the only link I had between Langritz and any of this whole crazy-ass situation. Maybe just something to keep in the back of my mind.

As I was pondering if I was nuts or not about Langritz and Delullo, my cell phone rang. It was Sharon calling with hopefully some information at Bartonelli.

"Hi honey, I hope you have something useful to contribute. I seem to be chasing my ass a little here and I need some direction."

"Not sure how much I have. I'm emailing you three pictures of Bartonellis who popped up on our databases. Why don't you pull them up on your laptop and give them a look?"

So, I pulled my laptop open on my dining room table. Started all the bells and whistles to get the thing going, and then opened my email account. I used a Gmail account for everything not Temple-related, and that's the one that Sharon uses all time.

I stared at the three pictures, but none of the three was my guy. They all looked pretty shifty, but they weren't my shifty Bartonelli.

I gave Sharon the news, "None of these guys are my guy. They all look a little scary, but not my guy scary. Which databases are these from?"

"I pulled up data from the Philly database, and also one of the federal ones at the Department of Justice. The National Criminal Information Center of the FBI is the most comprehensive, but that will take a little while to access."

"Well, we don't have a lot of time, but any info would make me feel better. So, does not finding this guy mean he's just a con artist or low-level thug, or we don't know yet?"

"We don't know, but I'm coming back in a few minutes. I'm bringing a very small camera that I'll set up outside your door next to the mailbox. Hopefully, we can get a shot of your guy tomorrow that I can run through the facial recognition database. That's really our best chance to get an idea on who this guy is."

"Any chance he might see it? That would be bad."

"Not likely, but don't forget I'll be in the back room monitoring everything. If anything goes south, I'll bring out the .45 and get his attention in a hurry."

I still wasn't completely sold on this plan, but I responded, "Okay, as I said, it's better to have a plan than not. When will you be back?"

"Should be about an hour. I'll set up the camera, and then we'll go out to get something to eat. Maybe a cocktail or two, but not too much. I'm sure you're ready to get some space between you and your house right now."

"Yeah, actually I'm ready to get some space between me and my house forever. Time to move to an island in the Caribbean."

Sharon chuckled, "Let's not make that call right now, but maybe keep it in mind for later. See you soon."

I hung up the phone and sat down at the table. I don't think Sharon's idea of "keep it in mind for later" really jibed with mine. Later was more like 45 minutes to me.

Chapter Thirteen

After she sat up the camera and taught me how to activate it with a small button in my pocket, Sharon and I had a nice dinner at an upscale restaurant in Center City. We had a couple of drinks but stopped at two because we both knew the next day was pretty important. We retired early, but neither of us could sleep. We got up and watched a Netflix movie for a couple of hours and then tried again. Sharon dozed off, but I just decided to read in bed. I finally went to sleep about two a.m., but even then, I slept poorly. We were both up by seven.

As we were drinking coffee, Sharon tried to set my mind at ease. "Look, I know this all seems pretty crazy to you, but it'll be okay. Trust me, I'm not going to let anything happen to you, honey."

"I know. I trust you completely, but yeah, this is a little out of my comfort zone."

"When he gets here, assuming he shows up, just tell him you think the money is great, and that you'll do right by him and his associates regarding FCL. In fact, given him a teaser if you like, and say that you did already did a quick look at FCL and you didn't see anything out of order."

"Okay, that works, I guess."

Since we had some time to kill, I decided to look through the FCL documents a little more, not that I was paying attention at all. Sharon had brought some other case files she needed to complete, so she just focused on those. It was pretty quiet for almost two hours. Then there was a knock at the door.

Sharon jumped up and hid in my kitchen. She couldn't be seen, but she could hear anything that was said. I opened the door, and sure enough, there was my buddy Bartonelli. I put my hand in my pocket for just a moment to start the camera.

Angelo was quick to get things started. "So, have you decided what you are going to do?"

I stumbled for a moment, but finally said, "Yes, I've thought about your proposal and I would like to accept your generous offer of $10,000. In return, I won't look too closely at the FCL tax and financial statements. In fact, I've already given them a quick look, and at first glance, everything seems kosher."

"Glad to hear it Dr. Stone." He took an envelope out of his jacket and handed it to me.

"However, I want to be clear that if you don't do what we ask, there will be problems. Big problems."

"I certainly understand. I'm just an accounting professor from Temple, and I'm not looking for problems."

"By the way, what about Lt. Levin? Does she know about any of this?"

"Of course not! When the documents were delivered, I told Sharon that I was very busy with schoolwork and wouldn't be able to look at anything for a while. As far as she knows, I haven't even started my review, and to put it simply, she doesn't really understand any of this, so whatever I find or don't find will stop with me."

"Well then, Dr. Stone, I doubt we will see each other again. Actually, for your sake, you should hope we never see each other again." And with that, he turned quickly and walked away.

Sharon came out of the kitchen, and just put her arms around me for a moment. I was taking in deep breaths and trying to calm myself. She said, "You did great! It couldn't have gone better, and let's just hope that he got some good pics from the camera."

I responded, "Why don't you go get the camera and see what we found?"

Sharon looked outside to make sure the coast was clear, and then she gathered up the camera. She brought it inside, rewound it, and took at look at what we had.

She did a quick survey of the recording and said, "We did very well. We got some good shots of your new friend, and I'm sure that once I have our techs work on them, we should have a good chance of having decent pictures to run through facial recognition. All in all, it went well. If you're okay, I'll head back to the precinct and start the processing to get the ball rolling."

"Sure, I think I'm going to try to take a nap. As you know, I didn't get a lot of sleep last night. Maybe I can doze a little to get back on my feet."

"That's a great idea. Lock up your doors and try to get some rest. I'll check on you in a couple of hours, and I'll give you an update on how things are going with the facial rec."

With that Sharon kissed me goodbye and left the house. I locked all the doors and just sat down on my couch. I wasn't sure if I was happy, or if I wanted to cry. It was a pick 'em.

Chapter Fourteen

I think I might have dozed for a few minutes. Not much, but it did seem to lift my spirits. I got up and made a cup of coffee, grabbed a bagel, and sat down to watch the news on TV.

I was sort of just staring at the box, and not really paying any attention. With all that I had been through in the last couple of days, tomorrow's weather was just not that compelling. Rain, snow, wind, whatever, didn't really seem to matter much in my new world of illegal activities, though I'm not really sure what those activities are. Just know they're probably not well.

My phone buzzed, and I saw it was Sharon. I answered and asked, "So, Lieutenant, do you have any good news for me?"

"I have some. The techs got a very good shot of your new pal, and we've started running it through the different databases: criminal, military, passports, etc. We're trying to touch all the bases, but I'm sure you can imagine that with all those data, it may take a while to comb through. The techs have set up the program to run overnight and to ping the night shift if a possible match comes through. Even with that, it may be tomorrow before we know if we have something, or someone. But we have access to a lot of databases, so it's likely Bartonelli will pop up on one of them."

"Okay, so what do we do now? Just wait to see what happens with the facial rec?"

"Actually, I think it might be good to get some takeout Chinese and sit and talk about what you're found so far. Might as well get a head start on whatever it is that you might have."

"I'm not sure there's much more I can add right now, but I guess it doesn't hurt to try. You're bringing over the food?"

"Sure, I know what you like, and I'll be over in about an hour. We can eat in front of the TV for a few minutes, and then you can give me a quick rundown of what you have so far. I may not understand all the technical accounting stuff, but maybe I'll see something of use."

"Sounds good to me. I'll see you in an hour or so. Don't forget the fortune cookies. Can't wait to see what mine says."

Chapter Fifteen

Sharon came over, and we decided to share the Chinese takeout. She got the moo shu pork and I got General Tso chicken. We set up some plates and split the food. I opened a bottle of Pinot Grigio, and we sat back on my couch to chill with some TV.

There wasn't much on, so, we decided to check out another old *NCIS*. I didn't mind watching cop shows right now, as long as the good guys win. And I had seen enough *NCIS* to know that they always do.

After we cleaned up from dinner, I spread out all the documents we had accumulated on my dining room table. There were not that many of them, but enough to make a nice little stack on each side of the table.

Sharon started, "So, give me the 30,000-foot view of what you have so far."

"Alright, here's the bullet. You know about FCL, Langritz, and Bartonelli. As I went through the documents, there are four shareholders in FCL, and I couldn't find anything important about three of them. The fourth guy, John Delullo, was in a bit of trouble back in the 90s and had to pay some pretty hefty fines. But he didn't do any time, and I couldn't find any new articles about any transgressions. Looks like he paid his fines and decided to keep a cleaner act, or at least a dirty one that is harder to find."

Sharon noted, "Okay, the Delullo name is new to me. I assume you just used the surface websites to get your info. I can connect to our Philadelphia criminal database from here and see if there's anymore updates on Mr. Delullo. I can do that when we finish here."

"That's great, and I hope you find something because things get a little thin from here. All I know from the Delullo articles is that he was involved in some land speculation similar to Langritz. Of course, there have been a lot of land speculators in the Philly area over the years, so there are a number of other folks out there similar to Delullo. I know, a tenuous link at best."

"Maybe, but maybe not. I've been doing a little research, too. Pulled up some old articles from the Inquirer and Daily News. Back when old Frederick was making all his dough, he had a reputation for being a very tough negotiator. So what? Real estate is a tough business. But, some of the articles suggested that Langritz played a little loose with the rules and danced around some issues that some might consider unethical. Naturally, once he made his first 10 mill, and made some generous donations to the orchestra and art museum, no one thought anything about any possible transgressions. Money can't buy you sainthood, but it can certainly make you saint-like to the masses. Even the Inquirer and Daily News jumped on the Langritz bandwagon and soon considered him a pillar of Philadelphia society."

"I was still down in North Carolina at that time, so I didn't know about that. I guess I'm not really surprised because most big money folks have something in their past. But I've got to say that I'm a little disappointed. I've always thought a lot of Langritz."

Sharon paused for a minute. Then she said, "Okay, bear with me for a minute. I may be going way outside the box here, but I have an idea. Maybe we need some more help in figuring this out. Obviously, I have access to all the law enforcement stuff, but maybe we need someone off the grid doing some investigating. And, I have someone in mind."

"Okay, can't wait to hear this."

"I think we might be able to use Matthew Scudder."

I sort of did the dog turning its head to the side bit. And then I responded, "Isn't that one of the protagonists for Lawrence Block, the mystery writer?"

"It is, but there really is a Matthew Scudder in Philadelphia, and he got the name Scudder long before Lawrence Block came along with his. The Philly Scudder was a cop for 20 years, but then he decided to get out of the bureaucracy of the police system and retired. He's been retired for a number of years now, and he's been working as a private investigator in the area."

"Okay, that's pretty interesting, but how do you know him?"

"I've had some contact with him with a couple of cases I've had. I needed someone who could ask some questions that cops can't really ask. And I needed someone who could do some things that would require a warrant for a cop to do."

I shook my head. "You mean to tell me that you, Sharon Levin, have been playing fast and loose with the judicial system. I'm shocked, shocked I say."

"Okay, I wasn't breaking any laws, though I might have bent a few, at least a little bit. But Matt, that's the name he uses, was a cop, so he does have standards and lines he won't cross. But he is interested in putting bad guys away, and after 20 years on the force, he knows what he can bend and what he can't. He would never put me in a position where his intel would cause a case to be tossed."

"How come I've never heard about him before? He sounds like an interesting character."

"He's never been involved in one of the white-collar crimes you've helped us with. He's really just a shoe leather kind of detective who knows his way around Philly."

"Well, if you think he might help, I'm all for it, but am I going to be on the hook for his fee? I don't mind if I am, but I sort of need to have an idea of how much?"

"Nah, I've done a few favors for him, and directed some work his way from other detectives, so I'm pretty sure that he'll help us gratis. Why don't I give him a call and see what his availability is like? It can't hurt."

"Sounds like a good idea because I'm a little stuck on what to do next. A new set of eyes certainly can't hurt right now."

"Then I'll give him a call and see if I can set something up for tomorrow."

Chapter Sixteen

Sharon called Matt and set up a time to come by my house around three today. I had my morning class but was done by 10 a.m. We decided to take a little break until he came by because we had really been working hard of late. Since we hadn't been down to the Italian Market in a long time, we figured it would be a good place to hang out for a couple of hours.

The Italian Market was originally named the 9th Street Market and dated all the way back to the late 19th to early 20th century. Italian immigrants began moving into the area and offered fruits, vegetables, and an assortment of meats in an outdoor setting. The name "Italian Market" became the name in the 1970s. As time moved on other immigrants moved into the area. Koreans, Vietnamese, and Chinese immigrants all came to the area and the choices of food expanded. But probably the most celebrated stores in the Italian market are Pat's Steaks and Gino's.

Pat's King of Steaks is credited with the beginning of the famous Philly cheesesteak. It opened in 1930 and began selling the cheesesteaks almost immediately. Gino's came along in 1966 across the street from Pat's. The two stores have somewhat different menus, but the staple of both are the cheesesteaks. Much is made of the competition between the two, but Sharon knew from the cops who work South Philly that it's a friendly rivalry. There is plenty of demand for cheesesteaks to support both stores, particularly on Eagles game day.

We decided to stroll the streets before we picked our cheesesteak location. While the vibe of the market had changed some over the years, it was still a very cool place to walk around. There were all sorts of nationalities represented and many types of food. Some of the meats and fish on display in the small stores looked as if they had just been slaughtered or caught. Fresh would be an understatement. Of course, there were a few people hustling some weird items like turtle and snake, but overall it just looked like a very interesting farmers' market.

I was starting to get hungry, so I asked Sharon, "So which cheesesteak brand do you prefer?"

"I think I want Geno's this time, because we went with Pat's the last time. Why don't we walk that way, and I'll decide on the wit or witout?"

I nodded, and we headed toward to Geno's. One of the things you need to do before going to Pat's or Geno's is the proper way to order a Philly cheesesteak. The basic choices are what type of cheese and onions or not? The choices of cheese are Cheese Whiz, American or Provolone. If you want Cheese Whiz and onions, you order is "Whiz wit." If you want one of the other cheeses, it's the same idea. If you don't desire onions with your Cheese Whiz, the order is "Whiz witout." This may seem a little ridiculous, but to the true South Philadelphian, and any other Philly fan, getting this right is a matter of civic pride. You've got to know how to address your cheesesteak needs in an appropriate manner.

As we walked toward Geno's, I also had to decide on my order. I generally liked a Whiz wit and some fries. Sometimes I step outside the box, but I'm a creature of habit when it comes to cheesesteaks.

The line wasn't very long when we got to the store. I let Sharon go first. "I'll have a Provolone wit, fries, and a diet

Coke," was her order. I responded with, "Whiz wit, fries, and a root beer." The counter person just nodded, and both Sharon and I felt pretty Philly with how well we had handled our ordering.

When the food arrived, we found a spot at one of the outdoor tables. We laid out our spread and proceeded to destroy our cholesterol level. Sometimes comfort food is the best thing for your overall attitude.

As we were scarfing down our food, I decided to ask Sharon questions about Matt Scudder. "So, how long have you known Matt? Was he a cop when you were on the force?"

"We overlapped by about a year or so. I was a very junior officer, and he already had his gold shield. We were in some meetings together, but we never worked a case. I was just above a beat cop, so our spheres didn't cross. Actually, many people were very surprised when he retired after 20 years, many stay longer, but the force had changed a lot during that 20 years, and Matt is an old-school kind of guy. Plus, I think he had been pretty cautious with his money, so the idea of working essentially part time as an investigator was pretty attractive."

"So, I know you can't really talk about cases you have worked with him as an investigator, but what do you think he can really bring to the party?"

"Matt has stayed clued in on the Philly cop world ever since he retired. He's also made some acquaintances in the so-called Philly underworld, too. He doesn't work for them, of course, but he has occasionally given them a heads-up on a possible upcoming bust. He doesn't do on it any big busts, but something pretty small, which wouldn't probably be a fine best case, he saves them the hassle of going through the courts and paying lawyers to do very little. That's gained him some cred in the shady community and sometimes they give him some tidbits in return. I figure he may have been able to gather some info on Langritz, Bartonelli, or Delullo that we don't have. May not do much, but you never know. We're not stuck yet, but we're also not making tons of progress. Sound okay to you?"

"Sounds great, but a lot of things sound great to me with a cheesesteak and some fries. Let's finish up lunch and head back to my place."

Chapter Seventeen

After lunch rather than taking a cab or Uber, we decided to just walk. Even though it was a bit of a hike, the fresh air felt great. We got back to my place on Rittenhouse about 2 p.m., and just decided to catch up on email and phone calls until Matt arrived.

At about 3:05, there was a knock at my door. I opened it, and a medium-build man, in pretty good shape, was standing at my door.

"Hi, I'm Matt Scudder. Sharon Levin asked me to drop by to discuss some investigative issues you might have."

I instantly took a liking to the guy and reached out and shook his hand. "I'm Ben Stone, and it's a pleasure to meet you. Please come on in."

Matt came into the room and came over to Sharon. "How's it going, Lieutenant" as he gave her a hug.

"Matt, it's been a while. You look great. Are you still riding the bike and lifting a little at your club?"

"Yep, trying to beat back Father Time if I can. You look good, too. How's the force treating you these days?"

"I'm keeping busy these days. Homicides in Philly are down, but there's still enough to keep us hopping. We're down a couple of detectives due to retirements and not being able to replace them. The mayor is always in the news talking about his commitment to public safety, but when budget time rolls around, he seems to forget that manpower and resources are the keys to safety."

"Sorry to say it, Sharon, but some things never change. It's one of the reasons that I decided to leave the force. Too much uncertainty with the City Council and budgets."

Sharon replied, "Can't really blame you, and it looks like semi-retirement is treating you well. What kind of cases are you looking at these days?"

"Believe it or not, I've gotten pretty good with the computer and spend a lot of my 'consulting' time at home gathering info about embezzlement, divorces, and other such things. I miss being on the streets some, and when you called, it really piqued my interest to try to get back out there. I know that you and Ben probably have all the electronic evidence that can be found. Plus, I know Ben is an accounting professor, so I doubt that I can comb the financials and find something he hasn't."

I nodded, but replied, "There's always something I could miss, but, yes, Sharon thinks that you could use a little shoe leather investigating and maybe help us out."

"I'm happy to help. Sharon has done me a couple of solids on work with the force, so I'm pleased to lend a hand."

Sharon decided to start us off. "So, I'm sure you know Frederick Langritz, so that's an easy one. The other two names we have are Angelo Bartonelli and John Delullo. I have some pictures of Bartonelli, but I haven't been able to get a hit on any of the databases. Don't know much about Delullo other than he's one of the shareholders in FCL."

Matt replied, "Langritz for sure I know, and back when I was on the force, there were the occasional rumor about he, shall we say, pushed the legal boundaries at times. Nothing big, and to be honest, nothing that almost every real estate investor gets shackled with. Also, I was pretty new to the force when he was in his heyday, but I did hear things sometimes. But, then, as you know, he hit it big, made monster donations to charities, supported the right people for mayor and City Council, so he became a hero. A somewhat reclusive hero, but a hero nonetheless. Can I get a look at the Bartonelli pics?"

Sharon handed him the pictures she had. "On first glance, I can't say that I know him, but he looks like a guy whose been around a while. I know some people I can ask about him. Don't recognize the third name, but Delullo is a somewhat common name in Philly, so I'll have to do some digging."

I said, "Well, we've made you copies of everything we have. I know you probably don't want to look through it all, but I'm an accountant, so I'm always about the data and getting as much as I can. Figured it wouldn't hurt."

"No, I appreciate it. You're right, I probably won't commit it all to memory, but it's good to have. I may skim some of it to catch some of the buzzwords for this type of business so I can look knowledgeable when I talk to people. Like you said, can't hurt to have more info."

Sharon inquired, "So where do you think you will start?"

"I still know some guys who are, shall we say, connected in Philly. Since Bartonelli is offering bribes and worse for Ben to not find anything, it smells a little like a mob-type gig. I've got some fellas who owe me a favor or two who are still in that loop. I'll see what I can find out from them, and then work from there."

Sharon replied, "That sounds like a great place to start. Ben can spend some time grinding the numbers, and I'll keep on the databases. We should also be getting more information from the crime lab which I'll share with you guys."

I handed Matt the files, and we shook hands. Sharon gave him another quick hug, and then he was off.

I told Sharon, "He seems like a really nice guy."

"He is, and he's a very good investigator, and he can knock on some doors that we can't. I think he'll be very helpful."

Chapter Eighteen

att got home and decided to comb through some of the FCL documents. He wasn't a lawyer or accountant, but he had seen a lot of legal papers during his time on the force, and actually had gone through a number of accounting files in his new role as private investigator. He really didn't think he would find something that Ben and Sharon had missed, but he figured if he had a solid familiarization with FCL, he might ask better questions.

As Ben had seen, the overall business strategy of FCL didn't make a lot of sense. Consistently overpaying for properties looked a little weird. But he had worked enough in law enforcement to know that there is usually a solid financial reasons for something looking strange.

Matt figured he'd handle Langritz himself, not that he really expected to find much, but for the other two guys, he might need help. He decided he might as well go ahead and start talking to people. Matt had an electronic Roledex on his phone. He knew a lot of people, but he had found that keeping track of them was not always easy. As he scrolled through his phone, he happened upon a likely source. Jimmy Tuboli had been born and raised in South Philly. Hardcore Flyers and Eagles fan. Also, as a teenager, he had gotten into some trouble early. Stole a few cars, moved a little weed, and scalped a few tickets at sporting events and concerts. Not enough to really get on the cops' radar scope, but then he got involved with the Philly mob doing a little extortion and loansharking. The stakes were going up, but Jimmy seemed to land on his feet, until he made a huge mistake.

There was a new restaurant opening up in Center City. It was a very expensive four-star place. Jimmy, on his own, decided to shakedown the owners for a piece of the action. The problem was that the police had figured something like this might happen, and they set up a sting operation. It went perfectly, and Jimmy got taken down on his first visit.

Since Jimmy had a juvie record, the extortion charge was going to have a pretty stiff penalty. Matt had known Jimmy for a number of years, and he had always liked him, so he decided to help him out. Matt convinced the D.A. that Jimmy had been helpful in a number of Matt's cases, even though that was totally untrue. In the end, Jimmy had to pay a huge fine and do a ton of community service, but he didn't do time. Jimmy had always appreciated Matt's help, so they had stayed in touch.

Jimmy decided to get completely out of the crime business, went into construction, made a little money, and started his own small construction business. He was still South Philly all the way, so he knew what was going on, but he stayed pretty clean himself. Matt decided that Jimmy was a good place to start. He punched in Jimmy's number on his cell phone.

"Yeah, it's Tubolli."

"Jimmy, it's Matt Scudder. How are you doing?"

"Matt, it's great to hear from you. I'm doing pretty well. Business could be better, but other than that things are good. What can I do for you?"

"I'd like to talk to you in person. How about lunch at Ralph's?"

"Whoa, Ralph's? Must be something big if you're willing to spring for Ralph's."

"Maybe big, maybe nothing. How about one o-clock? You got time?"

"For a free lunch at Ralph's, I'll make the time. I'll see you there."

Matt's decision to pick Ralph's was actually pretty strategic. Ralph's Italian Restaurant is one of the oldest eating establishments in Philadelphia. It was founded in 1900 by Ralph Francesco and has been in the family for over 100 years. It serves very traditional Italian cuisine, but it's considered by everyone to be great food. Plus, it clearly said a lot to Jimmy that Matt suggested Ralph's.

Matt got to Ralph's a little early to get a quiet seat in the back. He figured he'd get a house red because he knew his choice for lunch was the lasagna, and maybe a cannoli to wash it down.

Jimmy arrived a few minutes later. He greeted Matt with a big handshake and a hug. While they hadn't seen each other in a while, they still had a strong connection going back some years.

Jimmy opened with, "Well, you look good. Whatever you're doing with your semi-retirement seems to suit you well."

"Thanks, you look good, too. Seems that working construction keeps you in good shape."

"I'm doing mostly estimating and getting parts, but, yeah, I do still get out now and then to get my hands dirty. Gives me some street cred with the guys who work for me. Plus, depending on how much business there is, I may not be able to carry all my guys, so sometimes I need to jump in. I try to keep them all working as much as I can, but when we have a long lull, some guys jump to other jobs. But I think they all know I work very hard to keep guys on the payroll."

Matt replied, "It sounds like things are going well. Anyway, what do you want for lunch?"

"Same as you. House red, lasagna and a cannoli. Some things never change."

Matt asked the waitress to come over, and he gave her the order. She smiled because that was the go-to for many of the lunch-time customers.

Jimmy asked, "So what do I have to do to earn this luxurious meal? Bend some arms? Maybe move a little weed?"

"No, Jimmy, those were the old days. From the new and improved Jimmy, I just need a little information if you can find it. Do you remember Sharon Levin from the police department?"

"I met her a couple of times when I was engaging in less savory businesses, but I don't think I would know her. Why?"

"Her boyfriend is a professor at Temple. He teaches accounting, and sometimes he helps Sharon with some white-collar crimes. He seems like he's a really nice guy although I only met him once. Anyway, Sharon has thrown some work my way, so I told her I would help Ben and her out on a little issue that they have. You may have read there was a murder of a lawyer a couple of weeks ago. Anyway, there were some documents in that lawyer's office that found their way to Ben. Didn't seem like a big deal until a muscle guy showed up at Ben's home and offered him ten large to not look too closely at the documents. Guy also suggested that there were other, less gentile, methods to get Ben to cooperate. Needless to say, Ben, and even Sharon to some degree, was a little freaked out. They've done all the number crunching, and Sharon has run through the police databases, etc., but they don't really have a handle on what's going on yet. They asked me work the streets some and see if I could find out anything."

"Sounds pretty simple. What do you want me to do,? asked Jimmy.

"I've got two names and one photo that I would like you make some discreet inquiries about. The two names are Angelo Bartonelli, I have a picture of him, and John Delullo, a real estate guy."

"Okay, but what am I looking for with these guys?", asked Jimmy.

"Ben and Sharon both think these guys might be involved in some shady stuff, so I just want you to ask a few questions of some guys in the neighborhood. Don't push anyone too hard, I don't want you to get into any trouble. Just ask a few questions like you heard these guys are looking for a contractor, and you'd like to know a few things about them before you work with them. Nothing too deep, just a little info about how these guys operate."

"Doesn't sound too bad. I'll ask around a little, but you should know that I'm not in that loop as much as I was. Not sure if I'll be able to help that much."

Matt replied, "I know. I just figured it was worth a shot. Why don't we just enjoy our lunch, tell some lies about women, and bemoan how the Flyers are playing?'

Jimmy chuckled and said, "That sounds like a plan." just as their food arrived.

Chapter Nineteen

Matt knew that Jimmy was going to need a few days at least to see if he could find anything useful. So, Matt decided to start the Langritz deep dive to see if there was anything of interest there.

Since he had spent his life in Philly, Matt knew a lot about Langritz, just from reading the newspapers and magazines. He figured he might as well start with a Goggle search for a Langritz biography. He plugged the search terms into his computer and waited. Once the terms came up, Matt could see quickly that there had not been an authorized or unauthorized biography of Frederick Langritz. But there had been number of lengthy newspaper and magazine spreads over the years, although there had been much fewer of late. Matt decided to pick a couple of the longer articles to read mostly to refresh his memory.

As he perused the articles, there really wasn't much that was pretty common knowledge. Langritz started with nothing, became a real estate broker, got into real estate development, stopped developing to change to buying distressed properties waiting for the prices to jump. Made a fortune off the Convention Center, the Liberty Place complex, and the IBM center in downtown Philly. The only thing that struck Matt as somewhat strange is that Langritz never made a mistake.

Langritz was not the only land speculator in the city, but he seemed to be the only one who always scored a hit. Most of the other speculators batted about 50-60 percent success, but still ended up with some essentially useless properties.

But Matt found an article from the tail-end of Langritz's career that showed he didn't ended up hardly any real estate inventory at the end of his active career. The article, which was very complementary, just lauded how Langritz was such an astute investor. Matt thought for a minute that maybe that was part of the answer, but also thought that there were a number of very successful real estate speculators in Philly, but only Langritz batted a thousand. Maybe nothing, but worth a look. The question Matt had to answer was: How to look?

He decided to start online to see how far that could take him. He found rather quickly that the answer was not too far. While most of the recent real estate documents of late were digitized, the records for the Langritz heyday were still hardcopy and on file at either the Free Library or City Hall. While Ben and Sharon had really wanted him to hit the streets and see what he could find, it looked like he was going to be buried in musty old documents for a while. Well, at least he had Jimmy on the streets.

Matt decided to start with the Free Library. He drove his car over to the Ben Franklin Parkway and found a spot close to the Free Library. He had an idea of where things that he needed were, but he asked one of the librarians to help him out. She directed him to the second floor where the real estate archives were.

Matt asked the assistance of the librarian in that area which books he should look at to determine when certain houses were bought and by whom, focusing mostly in the late 1970s to the early 1980s. The librarian directed him to a large shelf of books on Philadelphia real estate transactions, and Matt pulled up the big volumes for the late 1970s.

He focused on transactions with Langritz and other real estate speculators he knew. Very quickly, he determined that the average holding time for the typical real estate speculator was five years. Langritz was about 18 months. And confirming what he had found earlier, Langritz never bought a parcel that he didn't flip to a real estate developer for a large profit.

Matt sat back in his chair at the library desk. He thought for a few minutes and then thought: How could Langritz be so incredibly and consistently successful? How could Langritz know which properties were going to be needed for development when no one else seemed to know?

And then it hit him: Insider information. But then where did it come from? Matt decided he had enough to hit the streets and try to gather some info about Langritz and his associates. City Hall and more musty records would have to wait.

Chapter Twenty

Since Sharon and Matt were both engaged with other activities, particularly Sharon who did have cases other than mine, I decided that I would look into the accounting and law firms associated with FCL. Figured it utilized my skill set, and since I was pretty caught up on teaching and grading, and didn't really feel like starting any research, I had some unencumbered time.

A quick look at Dreyfus and White's website only really confirmed what I already knew. It was a very old white shoe Philadelphia law firm. It had about 150 lawyers in Philadelphia, and about an equal number spread throughout the country and a few overseas. Much of their practice focused on defendant litigation, particularly the pharmaceutical industry. Looked like real estate was just a boutique branch that they provided for the more well-heeled clients.

The firm was almost 100 years old and had many partners come and go. I decided focus on the Langritz angle and the dates of 1970s to 1980s and looked for partners from that time period.

The Dreyfus and White website contained a tremendous amount of information about the partners, and while it took a while, I was able to get a pretty good list of the partners from that time period. I wasn't sure what it told me, if anything, but I felt good that I had accomplished something.

Next I moved to Teti and Associates. Since it was a small to medium-sized firm, it was much easier to comb their website. It had only been around since the mid-1970s, and the founding partners were about it until they expanded in the mid-1980s. Again, I wasn't sure what any of this meant, but it felt good to accomplish something.

Just as I was finishing up my feel-good session, Sharon called. "Hi, sweetness, how are you doing?"

"Not bad, just looking up some info about the lawyers and accountants involved. Got a lot of data, but not sure what it means."

"Progress not perfection. Anyway, I got a call from Matt. He's got a guy working the streets about Bartonelli and Delullo. Hopes to hear something in the next couple of days. He also did some research on his own. As we all know, Langritz was incredibly successful, but Matt looked at some real estate documents, and it looked like Langritz was almost too successful. He never made a bad move and always had his speculative properties bought out at a huge profit. Sort of like you, Matt's not sure what it means, but he feels like it must mean something. So now he's going to make some calls, talk to some people, and see if he can make headway with that angle."

I replied, "That sounds great. Off the top of my head, I don't know what it means, but it could be, as we say in the investigative mode, it could be a clue, just like my findings. I honestly don't know if we're making progress on anything, but I'm feeling better. How about you?"

"I'll feel a lot better if Matt and his buddy can come up with something about Bartonelli. He's the scary guy, and I would really like to have more of a handle on him. I'd feel a lot safer for you if we knew more."

"Well, Matt certainly impressed me as a competent guy, and your recommendation was outstanding, so if there's something to find, I think he'll find it."

"You're right, of course. Patience is not my strong suit. How about we go to dinner tonight and try to clear our minds of all this, and get a fresh start in the morning?"

"Don't have to ask me twice. Come on by the house, we'll pick a nice place, have a good dinner, and maybe we'll have something special for dessert."

"I hope I'm reading your inuendo correctly, and if so, I'm on my way. Make sure the sheets are clean."

"I always do!"

Chapter Twenty-One

Before Matt could really get started on trying to get a read on Langritz, he got a call from Jimmy.

"Matt, so I don't know if I have a lot for you, but I may have something. Wanna talk over the phone or perhaps we should meet?"

"Let's do it in person. I'm only getting started on my next angle so now is a good time. You want food or just a drink?"

Jimmy replied, "I'm not really hungry so why don't we just have a drink. Wanna hit the South Philadelphia Tap Room? I haven't been there in a while."

"Sounds great. I haven't been there in a while either. How about we head over there right now?"

"See you in a few minutes."

Matt didn't make it to the South Philly Tap Room often, but he enjoyed it when he did. The Tap Room had an amazing variety of beers and some great pub food. In fact, it had been written up in the Food Network's *Diners, Drive-ins, and Dives.*

Jimmy was seated when Matt arrived, and he already had a beer, so Matt asked, "I thought the drinks were on me? By the way, what are we drinking?"

"You can get the next round, and we're drinking Cape May Always Ready. It's pretty light, but it's got a very nice taste."

After Matt got his drink, Jimmy started in on what he had found. "So I made a few inquiries about the guys you are interested in. Not a lot on Delullo, at least from my end, but I asked around about Bartonelli, and the news isn't very good.

As you probably know, the Malino family used to dominate the Philly mob, but they've been replaced in the last few years. However, even though they've dropped a few places in the stats, they're still around and doing a fair amount of business. They've just really lowered their profile. Anyway, Bartonelli is an enforcer for the Melino family, and has been for many years."

"But why didn't he pop up on any of Sharon's searches and databases? Surely, he's got a record."

"Actually, not much. First, maybe some juvie stuff but that was probably tossed out. Second, he's just the muscle, so the cops haven't spent a lot of time on him. Even if they arrest him, he'd likely walk before sundown. Finally, he's actually pretty good at staying under the radar. A lot of his action over the years has probably been at night, no witnesses, just roughed someone up. To be honest, I'm pretty surprised that this thing with the accountant was done so out in the open. My guess is that whatever is going on must be pretty important. Bartonelli is usually way behind the scenes, so it must be a big deal of some sorts."

Matt replied, "You're right, this isn't good news. I've got to tell Sharon that she really needs to keep an eye on her guy. Not sure if it's enough for protective custody, but she and Ben need to be aware of this guy's history, and they need to be extra careful. Although, as long as Ben lays low and doesn't look like he's rocking the FCL boat, maybe Bartonelli will leave him alone."

Jimmy replied, "The only kink in that plan is that you need to find out Bartonelli's inside guy on the FCL investigation. I know you're keeping it all between you, Sharon, and the accountant, but things have a way of getting out. Wrong person finds out what you folks are doing, it could get ugly in a hurry."

Matt answered, "I know we need to stay away from Langritz which I why I've been library diving versus hitting the streets. I'm going to have to be very careful making any inquiries. By the way, are you sure your contacts about Bartonelli will keep their mouths shut?"

"Yep, I think it's cool. The guys I talked to thought I was just getting the low down on what type of guy he is because I was thinking about doing a job for him. I really didn't have to ask many direct questions, just bought a couple of beers, and let the guys brag about knowing a "made" guy. I seriously doubt that any of them will think anything about it. Just chatter at the bar."

"Okay, Jimmy, I really appreciate your efforts. If something comes up in your construction business where I might help, just give me a call."

"That's nice of you, Matt, but I still owe you for all you did for me back in the day. If not for you, I'd probably be in jail or dead. But I appreciate the offer, and I hope that this investigation thing works out okay."

"Thanks, Jimmy. Let's try to stay in touch more. Take good care."

Chapter Twenty-Two

Sharon and I were having takeout Indian food when we heard a knock at the door. In the interest of safety, I opened the keyhole and saw it was Matt. I opened the door and invited him in.

Matt started, "Hi folks, I was in the neighborhood and decided to take a chance and just drop by. I've got a little info about Bartonelli, and I thought it would be better to speak together versus over the phone."

I replied, "It's great to see you, but your opening sounds like I should be a little nervous."

"Unfortunately, that's the case. While I didn't find much on Delullo, one of my contacts, on good authority, discovered that Bartonelli is a wise guy for the Melino family and he specializes in the rough stuff. The reason Sharon didn't find him in the databases is that he's pretty good at plying his trade quietly. It sounds like things just sort of happen, and there's no evidence to incriminate Bartonelli. I guess the crux of the issue is that you two need to be careful around this guy. As you told me, Bartonelli must be tied to someone involved with FCL, because that's the only way he could have found out about your involvement."

Sharon asked, "So this fella has been in the mob for years, but we don't have anything on him at all? That seems pretty unlikely."

Matt responded, "I know that it sounds improbable, but my contact was pretty sure that this guy has been an enforcer for the Melino family for many years. Again, I think he's just pretty good at hiding his tracks. Plus, the Melino family isn't as big as it once was, so there's probably less action for him. Anyway, I guess the only real takeaways here are to be extra careful, and we need to find the link between Bartonelli and FCL. In that regard, I may have something."

I replied, "Let me guess, Langritz is involved?"

"Good guess, and it looks that way, but I can't be sure. I did some library work and found that Langritz almost never made a bad investment when he was making all his dough. All the other speculators won some and lost some, but Langritz batted a thousand. Now that could just be he's better than all the others, but it does seem unlikely. My next step is to ask some guys I know from back in the day if they know anything about Langritz's success in the 80s. It was a long time ago, and I need to be careful whom I ask, but I know a couple of fellas who might be helpful. However, I wanted to check with you two before I started down that road."

Sharon said, "We've tried to get something on Langritz, too, but most of it comes back as he was just a very astute investor. Maybe aggressive, but not really breaking any laws, but possibly bending a few. Might explain the FCL link to a degree, but not that much to go on. If you're pretty sure you can be discreet in your inquirers, I think we need to go down that road. Ben and I don't really have enough to start making any accusations."

Matt replied, "Then I'll call a couple of guys, and see if I can set something up. Both buys were in the carpenters' union, long retired, but were very active back in the 80s. I haven't heard from either in a while, but we used to be pretty close. We lived in the same neighborhood, watched the Mummers and Eagles together, and enjoyed a pint at McGillin's Old Ale House now and then. They may not know anything, but I doubt my questions will raise any suspicions with these guys. They just watch a lot of sports, go fishing down at the shore a few times each summer, and spoil their grandkids a lot. But I'll still be careful."

I replied, "Then I'll keep looking for a more solid link between the lawyers, accountants, and Langritz, other than just his name on a document. Maybe between the three of us, we can better piece together what might be going on."

"Then I think I have my marching orders, and I'll be in touch with you folks as soon as I have anything, if there is anything to have."

We all shook hands, and Matt left. Sharon reminded me, "Okay, Dr. Stone, we're going to do some digging, but I want you to be extra careful. If you find yourself in any tricky situations, you call me and my .45 right away."

"No problem, honey. I may know a fair amount about consolidated financial statements, but you definitely know more about center mass shots than I do. I've seen you at the range, and you can group them pretty well."

Sharon replied, "Keep that in mind, and don't do anything stupid that is out of your wheelhouse."

"Preaching to the choir, baby, preaching to the choir."

Chapter Twenty-Three

Since he found out Bartonelli is a pretty unsavory guy, Matt decided that he needed to get moving quickly. He looked up the names and addresses of the two guys he was targeting, Joe Knoblach and Bill Lester. His first call was to the Knoblach home, and much to his dismay, he found that Knoblach had passed two years ago. He expressed his sympathies to Knoblach's family, and then moved on to the Lester number.

He called the number and a woman answered. "Hi, this is Matt Scudder. I used to be a cop and now I work as a private investigator. I haven't spoken to Bill in a while, but I was wondering if he is around. I have a couple of questions about something from back in the day, and I thought Bill might be able to help."

"Hi Matt. I'm Bill's wife, Jenny, and I sort of remember you from a while ago. Bill is in the living room watching some hockey. Let me see if I can get him on the phone."

A few minutes later a voice came on the phone. "Matt Scudder! That's a name I haven't heard in a while. How the hell are you?"

"I'm doing pretty well. Retired from the police about 10 years ago and been doing a little private investigating on the side. Sorry I haven't been in touch more. Time seems to fly by, doesn't it?"

"That it does. No problem about not connecting, at least we are now. My wife said you have some questions going back a ways, and that I might be able to help. What can I do for you?"

"How about I take you out to lunch? Have you been to Dante and Luigi's recently?"

"Are you kidding? My pension doesn't allow for those types of places. I'm lucky to swing by Pat's or Geno's now and then."

"Then why I don't meet you there for lunch. Obviously, my treat."

"You don't have to ask me twice. I'll see you there about noon."

Dante and Luigi's is one of the oldest Italian restaurants in the U.S., opening in 1899. It's always been famous for its food, but also for Halloween in 1989 when an assassination attempt was made on Nicky Scarfo Jr., the head of a Philly mob family. A gunman dressed as Batman and carrying a candy bag opened fire on Scarfo with a MAC-10 machine pistol. Scarfo was shot eight times, but no vital organs were hit, and he returned home less than ten days later. That event has been seared into Philadelphia folklore.

Matt arrived at the restaurant a little early as he usually did, so he could get a prime seat. As he sat, he saw a much older than last time they met Bill Lester come in the door.

Matt stood, "Bill, I know it's you, but boy, do we both look older.

"That we do, Matt, but at least we're still kicking," said Bill as they shook hands.

"So, Bill, a little red wine to start us off? Maybe a house rose?"

"Sounds great. I don't drink that much wine anymore, mostly beer, but I still love a nice rose."

Matt ordered the wine, and then he started the discussion. "So, you retired from the carpenter's union about when I left the force. What have you been doing with yourself?"

"Oh, I did a little side work for a while, but 30 years in the union took a pretty good toll on my back and arms. I haven't done any side work in a while. The extra dough was good, but my body just got to the point that it hurt too much. I have to manage my budget a little closer, but it's better than waking up in the morning with pain everywhere. But, while I appreciate your efforts to catch up, you said you had a couple of questions for me. Why don't you go ahead and hit me with them?"

"Straight to the point, Bill. Some things never change. Okay, I wanted to ask you a few things about Frederick Langritz. You've heard of him, right?"

Bill responded, "The multimillionaire real estate guy. Sure, everyone has heard of him. Hard not to if you pick up a paper or see one of the art buildings downtown with him name as donor plastered all of it. Why do you ask?"

"I've been doing a little research on him for a friend. I know he made a fortune as a land speculator, but it just seems like he never made a mistake. All of his generally dilapidated spec buildings were all bought out for huge sums by developers for big projects. I recognize Rappaport did well, but even he missed now and then. I know you were clued into the real estate business through the union, and I was wondering if you had any ideas on how Langritz did so freaking well."

Bill sat quiet for a second. Then he said, "Look, Matt, that was a long time ago, but I can tell you a few of the rumors that went around. It was a great time for Philly real estate and projects were going up everywhere. We were all making a lot of money. But, you're right, Langritz was the biggest fish, and he was always right. However, most of those big projects were years in the making."

"The rumor around the union hall was that Langritz was tied into City Council and the Permit Division and got the heads-up on possible locations for big projects long before anyone else knew. Now, you would think that just meant that he was paying people off, but the rumor was that he had ties to the Melino family who really controlled City Council at the time. Any speculator or developer could get into a bidding war with Council, but the Melino ties made sure Langritz got the first look. When developers started looking at possible new projects, City Council and the Permit Division gave Langritz the info and he bought up a large number of parcels in one area. Then when the developers started looking for possible sites, the Langritz properties always came to the top of the list. And let's just say that the Melinos made sure that Council only allowed the Langritz parcels to be considered."

Matt sat somewhat stunned. "And no one did anything to stop this? The other developers didn't tell the FBI or cops or someone this was going on?"

"No one wanted to take on the Melino family at that time. They wielded a tremendous amount of power in Philly at the time, and it was in most people's interest to just play along. Most of the Langritz properties were in good locations, most of the projects were very successful, so the only ones who really made out were Langritz, the Melinos, and whoever was getting greased in City Council. It went on for so long that it just became the way things were done."

"I can't believe I've never heard of this. I also can't believe that the newspapers didn't investigate any of this and put it in the papers."

Bill shook his head, "Even the papers weren't going to go head-to-head with the Melinos. It just wasn't worth the risk. Plus, remember at the time the Melinos were almost folk heroes to many in Philly. Reporting on the Melinos would have probably driven their circulation down."

"Well, Bill, I certainly got a lot out of talking to you. Just so you know, I won't mention your name to my clients, just the facts."

"No problem, Matt. All of this seems like ancient history to me, but if it helps you with what you're doing, then it's fine with me."

Matt replied, "Then I think we should just enjoy our lunch and talk about how the Flyers aren't playing that well." With that he called the waitress over to take their order. But in the back of his mind, he was a little worried about the news that he had for Ben and Sharon.

Chapter Twenty-Four

It was early in the morning and I was sitting at my dining room table looking through my notes for my next class. I have taught these classes for a long time, but I still liked to review my lectures just to be careful. Accounting students can be very vicious if they think you've made a mistake. I have two or three in my morning class who love to play "prove the prof wrong." Actually, I really don't mind that much because I used to be the same way in some of my classes. My phone rang and I picked it up.

"Hi, Ben, it's Matt Scudder."

"Matt, good to hear from you. Got any information that might help us with this FCL mess?"

"Actually, I think I have some pretty important info, but I'd like to speak to you and Sharon in person."

"Sounds ominous, but okay. Sharon is at the precinct right now, but she's supposed to come by this afternoon with some papers for another case we have. Nothing as dramatic as FCL, but something we still need to do. Can you come over about 3 p.m.?"

"That's perfect. I'll meet you at your house."

Naturally, Matt's need to discuss things in person made me a little nervous. I called Sharon and gave her the heads-up that he was coming. She had the same reaction that it sounds a little worrying, but that we should try to stay calm until we heard from him.

Sharon got to my house about 2 p.m. and we looked at the other case for about an hour. We didn't make much headway, but sometimes the only way through it is through it. About 3:15 there was a knock on my door.

I checked the peephole as always and let Matt in. "Hi Matt, it's good to see you although it sounded like in your message that we're not going to like your findings."

"Good to see both of you, and yes, my news is not that great. Why don't we have a seat and I'll bring you up to speed?"

We all sat, and Matt started the conversation. "So, as you know, I spoke to an old friend of mine who was in the carpenters' union. To give it to you in a nutshell, he said that Langritz was involved with the Melino family back when he was doing real estate, and that they helped him pick the right properties for investment. He got some insider info about possible developments, bought the properties in an area, and the Melinos made sure that the developments were done on the Langritz land. He could hold the developers hostage a bit, and that's one of the ways he was seldom, if ever, wrong with his choices."

Sharon asked, "But how could this go unnoticed? Back in the day, the Melinos were very prominent and surely the cops, FBI, and media were all over this.

"I know it's hard to imagine, but, with Langritz, the Melinos were very careful. And other than some insider info, Langritz didn't do much with them. I sure some money exchanged hands between Langritz and the Melinos, but he kept his distance otherwise. And remember, the Melinos almost ruled City Council at that time, so any local law enforcement was going to get shut down quickly. They kept the whole thing all pretty neat and tied up, and the money just flowed where it needed to flow."

I inquired, "So do you think that Langritz is still involved with the Melinos?"

"It's hard to say. The Melinos' are just less prominent than before, but they're still around. If you can believe the papers, they've moved much more into the drug business and less in extortion, bribery, etc. that used to be their thing. A couple of their drug guys have been arrested and prosecuted, but they still have been successful at keeping the top folks under the radar."

Sharon asked, "So what would the FCL gig have to do with drugs? They don't need places to store the stuff, and why overpay for houses scattered throughout the Art Museum?"

We all paused for a moment and then simultaneously we all said, "Money laundering!!"

Sharon said, "That's got to be it. There must be a way they've figured out to launder their drug money through these houses, clean it up, and then use it for whatever they want. The question is: How does overpaying for houses really help them achieve their goals?"

Since I am the accountant and professor, Sharon and Matt looked at me with quizzing eyes. I thought for a moment, and then it sort of hit me. "All these properties are controlled by the Melinos including the overpaid for ones. They must, through some sort of shell corporations, also be the sellers of the properties. They don't care how much is paid for the properties because it's all their own money. They are overpaying to themselves to clean up the money and use it for whatever they like. FCL must be one of those shell corporations used to cycle the money through."

Matt added, "And they must need some legitimate shareholders to actually cycle the money through the banking system. It would be easy to do all this in cash, but that's a lot of cash to have laying around. I'm sure they have plenty of cash, but they need to get some of it into offshore accounts and the like to make payments overseas to their drug sources. No one really wants to send millions of dollars in cash down to Mexico or wherever. Money like that has a tendency to get lost at some point. Maybe that's why Langritz showed up on FCL."

Sharon said, "That makes a lot of sense to me, but going back to how this all started, why was the lawyer at Dreyfus and White murdered?"

I said, "If I had to guess, I would say that since he was very junior, maybe he asked too many questions about what FCL was all about. I'm sure that any of the partners at the firm would have quickly shut him down, but maybe he still kept looking at things. Maybe he sent the wrong email to the wrong person. I'm not sure why it became necessary to kill him, why not just seriously threaten him like they did me, but when you're dealing with a ton of money like this probably is, I'm guessing the Melinos might get nervous in a hurry."

"Well, I guess we have a working theory about what happened. I suppose that's a good thing although I'm not sure where to take it next," said Matt.

Sharon replied, "Matt, I think you've done as much as we could expect you to do. You've been incredibly helpful, and I owe you one on this. If you need anything, just let me know. And if I see any cases that might need your expertise, I will definitely send them your way."

"Sharon, I really appreciate that, and I was happy to help. I do have one request. If possible, once you and Ben figure this out some, can you keep me in the loop? I find myself a little intrigued with how this all went down."

"Absolutely, I'm happy to do that. It'll be by phone because I don't need to leave an electronic trail, but yes, I can keep you informed."

With that, we all shook hands and Matt left. Sharon looked at me and said, "Well, sweetheart, I suppose the next thing we need to do is figure what we're going to do next. Time to break out the Guinness?"

I looked at her. "Maybe more than one!"

Chapter 25

After we had downed a couple of choice Guinness beers, Sharon and I decided that it was time to talk.

I asked, "So where do you think we are? What do think our next step or steps might be?"

She replied, "Well, the problem is that we only have circumstantial, if that, evidence that Langritz was, and maybe still is, involved with all this. I don't have nearly enough to go to the District Attorney for any warrants. He would laugh me out of his office. Also, I could talk to my Chief, but I'd probably get the same reaction. All the stuff Matt told us about is long gone statute-of-limitations-wise. I'm not sure where we go from here."

Sharon sat and pondered for a moment, and then I could tell an idea came to her. She said, "I do have one idea, but it really depends on how much you and I want to clear this up. It's risky, and I'm not sure I want to do it."

"We're just talking right now, not making decisions, so go ahead and hit me with it."

"The key is Bartonelli. It sounds like he's been a made guy for a long time, and those guys don't roll on each other very often. But he's getting up in years and maybe taking the rap for a guy who is a prominent millionaire won't set well with him. I'm sure he's done okay with the Melinos, but I'll bet his house isn't a mansion in Gladwyne. That, of course, assumes we can get Bartonelli to believe that we have something important. To do that, we're going to have to do some serious bluffing. But that's the easy part in some respects. Maybe the hardest, and riskiest, part involves you getting Bartonelli's attention. Since you have no way to contact him, we have to assume Langritz was the one who got Bartonelli interested in you, and we'll have to play that card."

I replied, "What the hell are you talking about? You want me to get a made tough guy angry with me so he comes after me. That's your plan?"

"Like I told you, it's a risky and dangerous idea, but I can't think of any other way to make any progress on this. You've been through the documents many times and found little. I've combed through the databases, local, state, and national, and not found anything close to, to use the cliché, a smoking gun. I'm not necessarily saying I want to do this, and I'm happy to entertain any idea you might have, but anyway you look at it, it's a tough call."

"So let me understand this. We go out to Gladwyne, tell Langritz I've found some issues, figure that he or someone from his team tells Bartonelli about it, and then I wait for an enforcer to come to my house and enforce me. Yeah, that's not the best plan you've had."

"Like I said, it really turns on how much this matters to you. We could just let it go, keep the ten grand for a nice vacation, and call it even."

I thought about it for a minute. On the one hand, the path of least resistance seemed pretty attractive. On the other hand, a man likely died because of all of this, and my many years of feeling good about Langritz had done just gone out the window. That may have been the thing that was most exasperating about this whole affair. I'd held this guy in high esteem for many years, and now I find out that he was just a scummy guy using mob influence to make tons of money.

I turned my head back to Sharon. "Okay, I'm in. How do we make sure that Bartonelli doesn't kill me when he comes looking?"

"The last time we went to the mansion, it took only a day or so for Bartonelli to show up. If we're right and Langritz is the source of info, I expect it will move quickly again. Once we meet Langritz, I'm at your side all the time. I'll talk to my Chief and see if he will approve the time as a case. If not, I've got tons of vacation coming, and I'll just take the time off. Any way it goes, you're with me everywhere. You'll need to cancel your classes because I want to have complete control of your environment. We're going to hunker down in your house. I'll set up the camera again so we can see who comes to your door. No peephole, not that I think he's going to shoot you through the peephole, but I'm not taking that chance. I'll have my main .45, a backup gun, and plenty of ammo. Ben, I'm not going to let anything happen to you. I promise!"

Sharon and I had been in a few sticky situations before, but nothing even close to what this was about. I trusted her completely, but I was still nervous. This was a big step up from the little white-collar crimes I had done before. However, it seemed like we were going to do it, so we might as well start.

"Okay, babe, let's head on out to Gladwyne and see if we can catch some bad guys." I hope I sound more confident than I feel.

Chapter Twenty-Five

The next day we were very quiet on our way out to Gladwyne. There really wasn't much to say. The next couple of days were going to be very stressful, and possibly dangerous, and we knew that. Sharon had said we would discuss the plan for Bartonelli one more time when we got back to my house. So, we just listened to the news and drove in silence.

Since we knew the way to Langritz's house, we saved a little bit of time. When we arrived at his home, the gate was open, and we drove right up to the front door. Sharon rang the doorbell. The same butler as before opened the door.

"Can I help you?" he said.

"Yes, you may remember us from a couple of weeks ago. I'm Lieutenant Levin and this is Dr. Ben Stone. We would like to speak to Mr. Langritz again for a few moments."

"I do remember you, but like last time, Mr. Langritz does not appreciate impromptu meetings. You should have called and made an appointment."

Sharon responded, "That might be true, but we have some important information that we believe Mr. Langritz would definitely want to hear."

The butler said, "Fine, I will check with Mr. Langritz to see if he is free. Wait here."

Sharon and I just stood awkwardly at the front door waiting for the butler to return. We didn't want to say anything for fear Langritz might have listening devices around. It wasn't likely, but we didn't want to take a chance.

The butler returned, "Mr. Langritz is very unhappy that once again you paid him a surprise visit, but he is willing to give you ten minutes. Please follow me."

We entered the mansion once again, and once again, I was stunned by its beauty and grandeur. But, somehow knowing what I now know, it just wasn't as grand as before. To be honest, it made me feel a little angry.

We went to the same room and before, and once again, Langritz looked incredibly annoyed with us.

"So, you decided to surprise me again. I thought we had reached an understanding that this type of behavior is unacceptable. In addition, as I said before, I don't know anything about this case that you have, nor am I actively involved in whatever this is."

Sharon replied, "Yes, I recall our previous conversation quite well. However, Dr. Stone and I have some important information that we thought you might interesting. Ben, can you tell Mr. Langritz what we've found?"

"As you may recall, Mr. Langritz, there was a death of a lawyer downtown, and the FCL, Inc. documents came up in our investigation. The issue centered around some houses that FCL bought in the Art Museum area. It appeared that the houses were vastly overpaid for, and we were trying to figure out why."

"Yes, yes. I remember. I may be getting old, but I'm not senile yet, so I do recall. So what?"

"Well, sir, my analysis of the documents coupled with some interviews with knowledgeable sources suggests that money laundering might be the reason for the outlandish prices being paid for the properties."

"Money laundering! That's ridiculous! How does that make any sense, and why do you think I might know anything about this or even care. All of my money is perfectly clean, and I would never have the need for money laundering," replied Langritz.

Sharon said, "This is an ongoing investigation, so there are things that I cannot tell you, but we just thought that you should know since your name is on some of the FCL documents."

"Fine, you've told me. Now get the hell out of my house!"

As we got into the car, Sharon winked at me and said, "I guess that wasn't much fun, but the really hard part starts now."

Chapter Twenty-Six

While we drove back to my place, Sharon reiterated the plan. Her boss had given her the okay to be my shadow for four days. If it went longer than that, she would take some unused vacation. I was never to be without her, and I was not to leave the house at all. We had plenty of food in the house and Uber eats was always available. She had set up the camera outside my door, and I was to allow no one I didn't recognize into the house. If we got Uber eats, we would pay online and have them drop it at the front door. She would always have her gun at the ready in case we had any unannounced visitors. We would take turns sleeping to ensure any breaking and entering would be quickly discovered.

Nothing happened the first day, and then most of the second. We just took turns watching TV and occasionally doing a little work. Then late on the second day, there was a knock at the door. We were both awake, and Sharon went to the door to look at the camera. It was Bartonelli. Sharon took a close look at how his clothes hung, and she knew that he was carrying a gun. In fact, he had his hand in his coat pocket where the gun was located.

She told me, "I'm standing right behind the door. Open it a little and ask him what he wants. Just open it a crack and keep your shoulder braced against the door. Remember, I am right here."

Needless to say, I was shaking just a little, but I did as she told me. I unlocked the door and peeked out.

"Dr. Stone, I thought we had reached an understanding about FCL. I must say I am quite disappointed in what you have done."

With that, he pulled his gun from his coat pocket and started to raise it. Sharon threw open the door and put her .45 right into his face. "I would strongly encourage you to drop that gun to the ground. If not, I would be more than happen to put a couple of rounds right into your face. And don't think for a second that I have any hesitation in doing so."

Bartonelli looked shocked, but in addition he could tell that Sharon was quite serious. He dropped the gun to the ground. Sharon told him to turn around, she picked up his gun by the barrel, and then she had mo cuff him while she held her gun right at him. Once I had him cuffed, she had him come into my living room and told him to take a seat.

Naturally, the first thing he said was, "I want a lawyer."

Sharon replied, "Sure, we can make that happen, but first I think we should have a little chat. Since you've already lawyered up, you don't need to say anything, just listen."

"We've done a little digging and we know about Langritz and the Melino family. We know about the money laundering in the Art Museum area. But all of that is very trivial in your case. What I'm going to guess is that if I run ballistics on this gun, I'm going to find that it's the one used to kill the lawyer down at Dreyfus and White. That's going to stick you with a murder one charge, and I'm sure you know what that means. Life without parole."

Bartonelli responded, "You don't really have anything, and I'm not worried about what you think you might have."

"Well, you should be because I've got the smoking gun, literally, for that murder. You're going away for a long, long time."

Bartonelli hesitated for a minute and then said, "Okay, what kind of deal can I get and what do I need to do it?"

"It's pretty easy," said Sharon, "All you need to do is come clean about FCL and what they are doing. Oh, and you need to explain how Langritz is involved. Do those things, and we'll see if we can get you a little help from the D.A. and the judge on your sentencing. Whatever happens, you're going away for a while, but how long depends on how much you want to cooperate."

Bartonelli rolled his eyes and then said, "Okay, read me the Miranda, and I'll tell you what you want to know. Let's just do it here and get it over with. Here, downtown, wherever, let's just get it done."

Sharon smiled at me a bit, and then she sat down and read Bartonelli his Miranda rights. She had read suspects their rights many times, but she probably enjoyed this one the most.

Chapter Twenty-Seven

The next couple of days were quite crazy. After taking his statement in my home, Sharon had Bartonelli go down to the precinct and do it again. Her Chief watched the interrogation through the one-way glass. When she was done and walked out of interrogation, he just turned to her and smiled. He wasn't a very demonstrative type of guy, and a smile was a very big give for him.

The next day a warrant was drawn up for Frederick Langritz for conspiracy, money laundering, and even drug trafficking. The D.A. knew the drug trafficking wouldn't stick, but he decided to cast the net wide. The Philly cops, with Montgomery County cops assisting, went to Langritz's house and took him into custody. Not surprisingly, his very expensive lawyers had him out in about two hours, but he lost his passport and was required to wear an ankle bracelet. Given the resources Langritz had, the judge deemed him an imminent flight risk, and at first was going to deny bail, but Langritz's attorneys were quite persuasive that he wasn't going to run. The judge was somewhat persuaded but ordered the ankle bracelet, nonetheless.

Sharon took vacation for the next couple of days, and we just tried to decompress. We took some long walks, ate some great food, and watched a few movies. We also spent some time deciding which charity to donate the 10 grand to, and after a little debate it seemed appropriate to give it to the Philadelphia Fraternal Order of Police.

Toward the end of the second day, something came into my mind. I asked Sharon, "So do you think I need to worry about retribution from the remaining Melino family members over all this?"

"No, Bartonelli gave us enough on the Melinos that they will be tied up in court, and maybe jail, for a very long time. They've got much bigger problems than you right now. If something happened to you, that would only make life harder for them. Nah, you're good. You can go back to being your nerdy accounting professor self with the incredibly hot girlfriend."

"I'll take both. Love the incredibly hot girlfriend, but I never thought I would look forward to teaching intermediate accounting as much as I do now. Taking on a couple of aggressive students and snoring my way through some faculty meetings seems like Nirvana right now."

"I'm sure that's true. Also, I have to say that I'm proud of you, Ben. Not many guys would have taken the challenges and risks that came with this whole thing. I'm proud of you, and you should be proud of yourself."

"Thanks, and I guess I am a little proud, but I don't need to do anything like this anytime soon. Just teaching a few classes and pushing some papers around would be just fine for a while."

With that I kissed Sharon and we sat back on my couch and continued the decompression part of our lives. It was going to take a while, but I was sure that eventually I would return to being the nerdy accounting professor with the super-hot girlfriend.

Thank you for reading.
Please review this book. Reviews
help others find Absolutely Amazing eBooks and
inspire us to keep providing these marvelous tales.
If you would like to be put on our email list
to receive updates on new releases,
contests, and promotions, please go to
AbsolutelyAmazingEbooks.com and sign up.

About the Author

G. Steven McMillan is an associate professor at the Abington campus of Penn State University. Prior to joining academia, Steve worked in accounting and real estate in the Philadelphia area. He has received four Fulbright awards that have taken him to Finland, Belgium, and Malta twice. An avid traveler, he has visited over 30 countries.

Made in the USA
Middletown, DE
19 August 2020